My Perfect Wife, Her Perfect Son

Joe Benevento

My Perfect Wife, Her Perfect Son

Addison & Highsmith

Addison & Highsmith Publishers

Las Vegas ◊ Chicago ◊ Palm Beach

Published in the United States of America by
Histria Books
7181 N. Hualapai Way, Ste. 130-86
Las Vegas, NV 89166 USA
HistriaBooks.com

Addison & Highsmith is an imprint of Histria Books. Titles published under the imprints of Histria Books are distributed worldwide.

Library of Congress Control Number: 2023932043

ISBN 978-1-59211-201-2 (hardcover)
ISBN 978-1-59211-424-5 (softbound)
ISBN 978-1-59211-265-4 (eBook)

Acknowledgments

I sent a draft of the first chapter of this novel to a number of friends and family members, many of them writers themselves, to see if they thought I was off to a good start. Thanks to the following people who read those first pages and provided feedback and encouragement: Lee Slonimsky, Mark Belair, Jocelyn Cullity, Adam Davis, Joe Baumann, Prajwal Parajuly, Todd Rohman, Johnny Vines, Marjorie Justice, Michelle Terhune, Dave Smithson, Francine Tolf, Carol Benevento, Margaret Benevento, Joey Benevento, and Claire Benevento.

Particular thanks are due to Tom McGrath, Maria Benevento, and Kate Kort, who read the entire rough draft and provided generous and valuable suggestions for revision. I'd like also to thank Kate for her firm belief and assurance throughout the entire process of bringing my vision of St. Joseph to life on these pages.

Chapter One

Just as I stepped outside for a moment's relief I saw Mary walking toward my workshop and I knew something had to be wrong. Her house is more than a half hour's trek from my hut and the mid-summer sun was particularly intense that day just before noon, plus she had no chaperone. I quickly sent my apprentice out the back way to an early lunch then returned to look all around the dusty path to see if anyone had spotted her before hustling Mary inside.

The only place dustier than that dirt road was my work place itself, since there was still sawdust everywhere from the yoke I had been working on for a farmer's oxen. Mary didn't seem to mind or notice, even. I'm certain she was also unaware how anxious I felt whenever we were together, since I always did my best to hide it, but now we were all alone. Her unusually tall and graceful figure seemed only enhanced by her modest clothing – her blue-grey eyes capable of lighting up the dusky space we shared. Beyond her looks, Mary always amazed me with her gentle yet certain confidence. Still, I sensed some unusual urgency in the look she focused upon me, she who was usually so secure, so settled from her faith in the Most High.

"Mary, what are you doing here?" I asked as I cleaned off the one suitable chair in all that mess for her to rest upon.

"I'm sorry, but I just could not wait any longer. After all, our final ceremony is only days away." Mary refused the chair with a gesture and then said: "Joseph, I think it's you who had better sit down."

"Has your father decided to cancel the ceremony after all? Remind him we have a contract. These things aren't easily broken, even by a bigshot like him."

I took a breath, looked around my shop, a tired, messy hut, strewn with my work tools and three different jobs I was working on more or less at once: the half-finished yoke, a just varnished table and chairs, and off in the far corner where I did my metal work, a recently completed set of copper goblets. All that clutter certainly did nothing to calm my nerves. I was certain Joachim had finally decided he could go against his daughter's own wishes and prevent her marriage to a laborer, even though Mary had claimed the match was the will of the Lord himself.

"It's not my father, Joseph, not at all," Mary assured me. "It's, it's just that it's so soon before the ceremony and you still haven't said a thing. Hasn't he come to you yet to explain?"

"What does your father need to explain to me?" I asked, still full of suspicion.

Mary looked upwards, as if to search the heavens for how to proceed, but instead of a celestial sky, she saw only the dark, cobwebbed ceiling of my hut. She then looked me directly in the eyes and said with some exasperation: "Not my father, Joseph, not him. I'm talking about the angel."

"Angel? What angel?" I asked.

"The Angel Gabriel; I was sure by now he would have visited you too. It's been a month."

"Too? Too? So you're expecting me to believe you're getting called on by angels now?"

Mary looked at me perplexed, maybe even dismayed, but not at all ready to take insult. She stayed calm and proceeded:

"You must know me by now, Joseph, and so you know I'm incapable of telling a lie," Mary reminded me. "Yes, the Angel Gabriel came down to me, however unworthy I surely am. If you don't believe that, how can I possibly hope you'll believe the rest?"

"You mean there's more? My intended less than a week before the wedding is seeing angels and that's not the unbelievable part? Just what did this angel look like? And what did he want?" I asked, ready now, for the worst – or so I thought.

"Oh, he was so beautiful, Joseph, just as I always imagined, tall, in dazzling white robes and iridescent wings."

"Wings and all, eh?"

"Please, we're talking about the Angel Gabriel," Mary gently chastised my tone. "He appeared in my bedroom, maybe an hour after dinner."

"Some strange man just appeared out of nowhere and in your bedroom no less?" I questioned.

Mary did her best to continue to ignore my tone, though she maybe was starting to look a little worried. "I was in my room praying when I heard a voice behind me say: 'Hail Mary.'"

"'Hail Mary?' Why did he say, 'Hail,' Mary? Jews don't greet people that way, Romans do. Are you sure he didn't say, 'Shalom Mary.'"

"No, it was 'Hail,' definitely 'Hail,'" Mary insisted.

"Well, this was no Jewish angel then. This was some Roman disguised as an angel, or better yet some demon," I decided.

"Please, Joseph, just listen. It was my mistake to come here, I should have waited for the Lord to do his will in his own time, but now that I've begun, I must explain it all to you."

I was certain that my lovely bride-to-be had finally gone crazy from all the praying and reading and fasting and those early years practically living in the temple, as Joachim and Anne's thanks to the Most High for having finally blessed them with a child. But what could I do but hear her out?

"He said to me, 'Hail Mary, full of grace. Thou art highly favored, the Lord is with thee. Blessed art thou among women.'"

"You remember this all word for word?" I questioned with a shake of the head.

"When an angel speaks, you listen," she replied. "Maybe I've mistaken a word or two, but mostly it's like a beautiful dream that keeps playing over and over in my head, with the words always the same."

I knew Mary had always sensed somehow that she was meant especially to do the Lord's bidding, but now I could only guess her desire for special favor from the Most High had carried her away to this fantasy. But there was more, much more.

"Of course, I was amazed, not only to find an angel in my bedroom but also from this strange greeting. He could tell I was confused, so next he said: 'Fear not, Mary, for thou hast found favor with God. And behold, thou shall conceive in thy womb and bring forth a son and shall call his name Jesus. He shall...'"

"What's this Jesus business?" I interrupted. "What kind of a name is that? I was thinking Jacob or Heli or maybe even David for a boy. Besides, we haven't even taken up house together. How can this Angel be so sure?"

"That's exactly what I asked," Mary nodded. "And the Angel replied: 'The Ruach ha-kodesh, the Holy Spirit himself, shall come upon thee and the power of the Highest shall overshadow thee: therefore also that holy child which shall be born of thee shall be called the Son of God.' And that's exactly what has happened to me, Joseph. A blessing and a miracle, as I am now surely with child."

Mary had been right to make sure I was the one sitting down. Somehow the combination of the heat, the close quarters and especially what Mary had just said made me feel light-headed and weak and even sick to my stomach. And these physical ills prompted me to consider that maybe Mary wasn't really crazy. I now began to suspect baser things.

"You're telling me you're pregnant? Who is the father? How could you do this to me? This will destroy your parents. And aren't you afraid of the high priests and rabbis?"

I paused but Mary stayed silent, as if she could be surprised by my reaction. How else could a person react? I waited another moment but then kept on:

"Better yet you want me to believe it's the Holy Spirit who made you pregnant? And if that weren't enough you're going to birth the Moshiach himself and to top it off said Messiah is actually going to be God's son?!"

With each sentence my voice got a little louder, more strident, so that I was practically shouting at her by the end, I who have always treated Mary with respect and affection and a little awe. But how much is any human being expected to bear?

Mary tried to calm me down: "This will take great faith, Joseph, but, yes, we are blessed beyond belief. I am to bear God's child and you are to be his father on earth. It's an incredible gift the Lord has bestowed on us."

"Where are you getting all this from, Mary? We don't believe in people conceiving with the gods – that's the Romans, again. You know we believe in the one true God and he isn't a rascal like those pagan gods. I knew nothing good could come from your father consorting with those Romans so much in his businesses. And more than a lie it's blasphemy to say you are carrying God's child, an incredible insult to me your betrothed, and an absolute rejection of our most sacred scripture."

Tears were now in Mary's eyes but instead of consoling her I got up from my chair and began to walk away. She came right up to me and refused to be ignored: "No, Joseph, there's no sacrilege, it's right from our own religion, from the great prophet Isaiah himself who says: 'The virgin will conceive and give birth to a Son and they will call him Immanuel.' I swear to you I am still untouched by man."

"If that's so then you can't be pregnant," I tried to reason.

"But I am with child, Joseph, though I've known no man. I've already begun to have the morning sickness. That's why I was impatient to discover if the angel had come as yet to you. He will come, he will explain all, but for now your love must be strong enough to believe. I am faithful to you, but I am, as I said in parting to the Angel Gabriel, 'the handmaid of the Lord'; I will suffer anything to do his holy will."

What could I say to her? She was crying; my disbelief had upset her, maybe even surprised her. For her own predicament there were no tears; I could tell she was completely convinced all this nonsense was true. Had some Roman raped her and this was the result, a descent into madness? In my mind it was too much of a leap from the Mary I felt I knew to believe she had willingly made me a cuckold. But of course even if she had been assaulted I couldn't go forward with the marriage; I knew that at once. I wasn't equipped to deal with a mad woman who would want to raise her half-Roman son as if he were some sort of deity. But this was no time to let her know. I'd want to be sure the contract could be broken without shaming her or causing her harm. If it was more than she deserved, if she somehow had fooled me all this time – with a devout charade – that would be on her soul, not mine.

"So, Mary, I too am to be visited by the Angel Gabriel? I'm sure he's been busy, the world is such a mess, but I expect he'll come soon and then I'll be better able to understand all this?"

"Joseph, I can tell you still don't believe, but, yes, exactly that will happen and all still will be well – so much better than well – the honor we have received is unprecedented in all the history of our people. Oh, and I almost forgot, the Angel also told me that my cousin Elizabeth is six months into her own pregnancy, and that was a month ago. Right after our ceremony, I'll want to go and stay with her to help out."

"Cousin Elizabeth? Isn't she almost fifty? Didn't she and her husband give up years and years ago? Then again, if you can believe in virgin births, old barren women's births are no big deal, I suppose."

Mary again understood but ignored my sarcasm. She even had room for a half smile as she seemed ready to exit the hut: "Your doubts will all be washed away, my beloved. The Most High chose you as surely as he chose me so I know you will come to believe as fully and as gloriously as I do. The Most High has tested me today for my impatience, but his eternal wisdom cannot be forestalled by the restlessness of a foolish girl. Farewell, my beloved. I will see you tomorrow at my father's house for dinner."

Mary has some vocabulary; all that reading has made her the closest thing to a female scholar anyone in Nazareth has ever beheld. But all that fluidity of speech and her restored confidence could not change what I had to do: figure out a way to put her away quietly, without upsetting her rich parents, without causing the community to condemn her. My hope was that she was not pregnant at all; she certainly wasn't far along, in any case, but for a virgin to make up such a story still was bad enough. The Angel Gabriel! The Holy Spirit plus the Most High Himself! I knew it was all too good to be real, that I, a struggling craftsman should get to marry so rich and so well, and to a woman who was more kind and gentle than her parents were rich. That was what I should have realized was unbelievable all along. And now I could see no easy path to getting out of this unbelievable mess.

***

The rest of the work day I was useless, making more mistakes in three hours than I usually make in a month. I sent my apprentice home early, which made him even happier than his early lunch break, and I washed up and went home. Back in my bachelor days, "home" was just a side room attached to the shop, where I prepared my meals and slept on a mat, but after my engagement to Mary, Joachim and Anne had both decided that no daughter of theirs was going to live in a hovel. They insisted I build a house for when Mary would come to live with me, which would have been months ago if not for the usual delays that come with construction. Of course framing the house was not the hard part, but it all had to be just so to please them, inside and out. I had also to build a bed for Mary who wasn't accustomed to sleeping on a mat, and for the walls of the home white wash wouldn't do; every room was painted a different shade of Mary's favorite (and most expensive) color, blue, with paints Joachim had to import from Egypt. Of course, I had been enjoying the comfort of the new dwelling for the past two weeks, but now all I could think about was how I was going to rid myself of this trouble without getting in an even bigger mess with the Rabbi and my almost-in-laws.

After a simple dinner of a little goat cheese and olives and a few figs, I said my evening prayers and tried to retire early. Of course it was a mistake; I fretted fitfully for hours and then began a series of bad dreams. Like my namesake, I've always dreamed a lot, but I've never had the skill or even the need to try to interpret them. One was unambiguous, though; I dreamed Mary was being stoned by many people I did not recognize, but then, most horribly, by her own parents. This dream unsettled me, made me somehow feel guilty, though I had done nothing wrong. I got up to splash water on my face; I was sweating like a shepherd. When I approached the water basin, I had the strange feeling I was not alone. I didn't have long to realize how right I was.

"It's about time you woke up. Joseph the craftsman, am I right?"

"Who's there? Who is speaking?" I asked with alarm, as I heard only a voice in the darkness. Suddenly the room was illuminated by a kind of purple cloud suffused with light, but then the cloud took form, though the light stayed, along with a man in my bedroom. Cloud men are by no means an everyday occurrence, but I had been told to expect an angel, so I was not entirely afraid or astonished. Once I was able to focus more on him, though, I knew this was not the Gabriel Mary had described. He was short, with dark, receding hair that looked unwashed. His spindly legs and dirty sandals were not hidden by angelic robes and he had dark eyes and a prominent nose that reminded me of my own, except his was adorned with more than one mole. More disturbing still, there were no wings. He seemed to read my mind:

"I'm no cherubim, Joseph. We first-rankers don't need to sport wings, though Gabriel loves to show off," he explained to me in an at once loud and raspy voice. "That's what wings are for – just for show – something to look impressive in the temple drawings. It's not like we need them for flying or anything. I get around fine without wings, I can tell you."

"Never mind the wings," I said, perhaps a little rudely, considering my possible audience. But how did I know this was an angel and not just an intruder from off the street? "I just want to know who you are and what you're doing in my house," I insisted.

"Don't be coy, Joey; you already know why I'm here. It's all over paradise that she told you already. Couldn't wait till I got here – just like a woman, am I right?"

I think I tried a look of disbelief, but how was I going to manage it? This purple cloud man seemed to know what was up.

"So, it's true? Mary is with child yet, she is still, a, you know, a…"

"A Virgin? Yes, of course, absolutely. And I can tell you, confidentially, mind you, that she will be celebrated as the 'Blessed Virgin Mary' for all ages to come."

"The 'Blessed Virgin Mary'? You've got to be kidding me. This cannot be on the level." I said as I backed away from the angel, almost tripping myself on the foot of my bed. "And why is this happening? And why am I involved? Mary, everyone knows she's a holy one, but, me, a poor craftsman, what do I have to do with any of this?"

The angel laughed, a most human laugh, quick and almost derisive. "You can ease up with the 'poor craftsman' routine, Jo-Jo. I come from the Most High, remember? We know you do a pretty decent business – Joseph the craftsman – woodworking, stone masonry, even metal work you've added – you're no ordinary laborer. Plus you know your Torah too. Sure, the Lord wants his son to have humble origins, but not too humble and definitely not stupid. Proper nutrition, a stable home, knowledge of the holy law and keeping with all the observances: these are necessary for the development of any good Jew. Sure, the Moshiach is to be the son of the Most High, but he's also supposed to be a person, if you can wrap your head around that one."

I looked at this so-called angel, so glib, so unlike the way Mary had described Gabriel and I wondered if he were instead a demon, sent to bedevil me for my many sins. I looked him in his dark eyes and said: "I can't be part of this insanity."

"Can't is not in the Lord's vocabulary. Just ask Job or Jonah or any number of the prophets. So it *can't* be in yours either, my craftsman friend."

"You mean I can't say no. You're going to force me?"

The cloud man shook his head. "Again, Joe, who are we kidding here? Everything is preordained, like you being House of David and all that. You're not *the* chosen one, but you've been chosen just the same. Of course, what I mean, though, is that you'll freely choose to say yes. I know, that's a tricky one too. But go ahead and marry Mary and just trust in the Lord. That's the simplest way, am I right?"

He seemed somehow like he was getting ready to depart, something in the way he said those last words. I almost grabbed him by the arm, but I wasn't certain that was allowed, so I said instead: "That's it? That's all you've got for me?"

"Hey," he answered, "this is nothing. It's going to get worse before it gets better – count on it. But you look pretty strong to me. You'll do the right thing; I'd put some shekels on it if we had money up where I come from. God is no crazy man – he knows who he can count on. Good luck Joseph. Shalom."

With that the angel became once again a cloud, a light purplish cloud, and he disappeared before I even learned his name. What happened next, though, was even more disturbing. I woke up. I had never actually left my bed, never gone for water. It had all been a dream, which explained, of course, why my angel had been such a wise guy. And dreams aren't real. So it seemed I had had no visit from an angel at all. So now what was I supposed to do?

Chapter Two

The very next day, I was scheduled to have dinner at Mary's house. It was going to be the last time before the ceremony that I was to see her, and her parents wanted once more to go over all the details of the ceremony and celebration they had so carefully planned. I would have preferred to spend the day figuring out what I should do, perhaps confide in my best friend Jude who was to stand for me at the ceremony, since I had no family in Nazareth and my one living brother no interest in making the long trek for the wedding. But what was I supposed to tell Jude? Or anyone for that matter? I still was far from100% certain Mary was pregnant, and if she was I had no idea from whom or if anyone would believe it wasn't from me. Her parents were the most powerful people in all of Nazareth; lots of people owed their livelihoods to Joachim's many farming and business interests. I needed time, but there was no time. I spent another unproductive day at work, once more let my apprentice off early (he was starting to get suspicious, I could tell, but was too happy about leaving off work to be very inquisitive), and got ready for the long walk to Mary's home.

The house of Joachim and Anne was easily the largest and most elaborate in all of Nazareth. Constructed of the finest hewn stone from Joachim's own quarry, there wasn't a single mud and straw brick in the whole two-story structure. It was the absolute pride of the town. Inside there were beautiful mosaics adorning some of the inner walls and during meals one sat not on mats or cushions on the floor, but at a wooden table with wooden chairs. I myself had constructed that table and those chairs, as part of my end of the dowry, and from pistachio wood of all things, because Anne had seen a bowl made from pistachio and decided she had to have a dining room set of the same wood, which was not only difficult to obtain but also devilishly tricky to work with. I'll admit, though, the final product was both unique and beautiful, with natural color ranging from olive green to almost violet, with dark brown stripes throughout. Happily, it seemed to be holding up to daily use even better than I had hoped for.

Though the food was always plentiful and delicious and though Mary's mother was one of the few people in Nazareth who had servants to help with its preparation, I never enjoyed any meal there. Both Anne and Joachim tried to act as if they were not proud to have wheat bread instead of barley loaves or a guinea fowl for a mid-week dinner that many of their neighbors could not manage even for a holy day, but you could always tell that they were noticing how much you were noticing. In fact, they were very particular people. This was why they had expected their only child to do better than a common craftsman for a husband. Of course, my being without a family of my own in town did make it easier for them to get their way in every aspect of the upcoming ceremony.

"So it's settled," Anne announced, though I had been too distracted by worry to notice what she had been talking about up to then: "The wedding feast will feature not only lamb but all kinds of poultry, including pheasant, and for a crowning touch, peacock, which wasn't easy to get, I can tell you."

"Mother, there's no need for such extravagance," Mary protested in her quiet way.

"Daughter, you must let us have this celebration. We are inviting the entire town to share this joy with us, so the richer the food the more the Most High will bless your union," her father concluded. He then turned his attention to me.

"So, I guess you don't think we're being too extravagant?" he asked with a dry chuckle. "I know you'd like a chance to try peacock and the other delicacies. And why not?"

"Yes, Joseph has a good appetite," Anne agreed. "Though you've hardly touched the food before you. You're feeling all right aren't you?"

"Not maybe having second thoughts?" Joachim asked and the question sent him into a near spasm of laughter. "Not wanting to get out of marrying the finest catch in all of Galilee?" he continued the joke. "No, woman, he's not sick; he's just anxious for the real feast in a few days," he concluded. I nodded pretending I appreciated Joachim's humor, but of course, all this talk of the upcoming ceremony just made me more frantic. No matter how long I lingered after dinner I found no opportunity to talk to Mary alone, nor did I know what I would have said to her if I had had the chance. Mary seemed back to her normal, calm self and I'm certain she took my attendance at her house as a sign that I now was on board with being the Messiah's stepfather. I worried that she might feel so confident in me that she would next announce the results of her visit from the Angel Gabriel to her folks. After all, they had a great reputation for piousness themselves; they would be a lot more likely than me to want to believe their precious daughter was going to deliver the Messiah in about eight months, give or take. But I guess it was our secret for now. I was saying my farewells without having resolved anything with Mary, though in my own head and heart, it was just a matter of when, not whether, I should disengage myself from this fancy family and their crazy daughter.

A long walk awaited me, but I figured it would be a good opportunity to plan out what I would say to the Rabbi, but maybe half way home, I was startled to realize that it had begun to rain, something most unusual for mid-summer in Nazareth. The rain was steady and surprisingly cold, but there was nothing to be done but to keep walking, even though I hate to get wet with my good clothing on. If the rain were not enough to torment me, next I thought I discerned a large figure at some distance directly in front of me. Robbers were fairly rare within our town but not unknown, and I had only a lantern with which to defend myself. As I got closer, though, I realized through the raindrops that the shape I was seeing was not human. It was instead a camel I was approaching, one without rider or keeper. I assumed it had gotten loose from some merchant or trader and I expected to pass it without incident. All this changed when I approached the beast on the fairly narrow road and it turned and blocked my path, as if on purpose. Each time I tried to sidestep the animal, it moved in the direction needed to continue obstructing me. I was so tired, upset and confused that I considered giving its nose a good strike with the lantern. It seemed to read my mind, turned its head towards me and tried to spit right in my face.

When camels "spit" what they're really doing is regurgitating their cud, mixed with some saliva, and then letting it loose at whatever unlucky man or animal has offended them. Knowing the way of camels only too well, I dodged just in time and readied myself for its next aggressive move. Of course, an angry camel is a formidable foe – it charged me and butted me and before I knew it I was on the ground, the wet, messy ground, with my good cloak covered in mud. I slipped twice as I tried to get up, righted myself and reached for my lantern so I could strike back. Instead I was struck when I heard a strangely familiar voice cry:

"Don't even think about retaliating, craftsman. I'm angry enough already without that."

There is an expression one uses for a sweet, soft-voiced female, the "voice of an angel," but this was the voice from last night's dream, deep, coarse, sarcastic and now angry. I prayed somehow that it was just a drunken delusion, but remembered I had had only two cups of wine the entire evening. Still, this camel knew whatever I was thinking: "It's not the wine talking, Joey-boy, it's me, the Angel Shlomo, and I'm losing my patience with you."

"Shlomo?"

"Well, Solomon, of course, but I prefer Shlomo with my friends. I'm still hoping we can be friends, but you've got everyone pretty upset."

He was a better looking camel than he had been an angel. My lantern revealed two healthy humps, a beautiful, well-groomed pale tan coat and deep, but peaceful dark eyes.

"There's no mention of an Angel Solomon in the holy books."

"Doubts? That's what you're giving me, doubts? Are you crazy or just stubborn? The Most High has delivered the rain in mid-summer, I've come to you as a talking camel – are these the ordinary events in a craftsman's life?" he thundered and stomped his right front hoof for emphasis.

"I should be grateful then?" I handed him back some anger, even as I tried wiping the mud from my beard.

"None of your sarcasm, craftsman. It's not for you to question or comment, but to believe. We want men of faith. You've failed on the first try. But since Jonah got a second chance, and since what we're asking from you is much harder to swallow than Jonah was, I'm here to convince you, and all you are suffering is a little rain and mud."

"You could still be a demon. Whoever heard of an Angel Solomon?"

"I prefer Shlomo," he insisted.

"How do I know you're not a demon? How do I know that Mary's child is not a demon child? I've heard that the seed of newly dead men is used at time by devils to impregnate young virgins. How do I know this really is the will of the Most High?" I shouted.

"Do the right thing, Joseph. I can read your heart and know these are not true doubts, just excuses to resist the will of the Most High. I can't promise you'll never regret it; as Mary told you, Angels cannot lie. But at heart you are a good and worthy man. You have been blessed and will be blessed for all time. Don't refuse your fate. You won't receive a third opportunity."

With these last words the camel-angel-cloud vanished quickly as in a dream, as if he had never really been there. The rain also had stopped. The mud on my cloak was gone, as too the bit of camel spit I had discovered in my hair, a gross mix of water, dirt and angel anger. I found myself laughing, not the laugh of a happy man but of one who has lost his mind. So this too had been but a dream, a walking, waking dream, but though unusual, it was not as hard to believe as an actual angel-turned-camel or even rain in mid-summer. Maybe the mix of wine, anxiety and worry had caused it to occur. Just as I had settled on that as a saner thing to believe, I felt more cold wet weather falling from the sky. So, the rain at least had been real, I figured. But when I looked up to see the clouds, I saw instead a clear sky, immense and full of stars, with one star brighter than all the others, a star of blue fire, seeming to follow me as a walked. And when I used my lantern the better to see the rain on my cloak, I saw instead white flakes, no two alike. It was snowing, just on me; wherever I side-stepped the snow followed. But the snow was fresh and clean and the star said not a word yet spoke to me of faith. And this shining star, in Mary's favorite color, and this personal snowstorm in mid-summer, were a little too much to doubt. This too had to be a dream, but what did it matter? Nothing was impossible, after all, for the Most High.

Chapter Three

Custom dictates that the bride should not know the exact hour or even day when her groom should come to fetch her to his own father's house, to begin the final steps of marriage, the nissuin that would end in a week-long celebration of the new couple's union. Of course, as an orphan I had no father's house to leave from, but instead the house Joachim had insisted I construct. And no one was going to take Joachim and Anne's daughter by surprise, so they had laid out for me exactly when I should arrive to "surprise" her. As was fitting, I arrived in as fine array as a crafts-man's labor could manage, in a beautiful scarlet robe that Jude, my best and really only true friend in Nazareth had fashioned for me himself in his tailor's shop, refusing to take any payment from me, beyond the cost of the cloth itself. He said it was his wedding present and his work was certainly worthy of a king. Of course, no matter how well I was dressed, I could not hope, nor even desired, to compete with my bride. She, surrounded by servants and bridesmaids, looked more beau-tiful than life itself in robes of white and blue. All of her retinue came out at once, and Mary boarded the litter that was to carry her in splendor and song through the streets of Nazareth to my door.

Once they all arrived at what would be our home, I was of course to leave Mary to her attendants and the ritual cleansing and other preparations before she could actually see me again. I decided to stay out of the house entirely and spent the hours with Jude, whose calm demeanor would normally have been enough to help any new groom, but of course I hadn't been able to confide in Jude my additional trauma, the secret of Mary's possible pregnancy and its heavenly cause. I still felt I would have to be a madman to actually tell someone, even a close friend that I was being asked to believe all this. And of course it's a funny thing, faith is. I had decided some combination of my regard for Mary's kindness and purity and the strange waking dreams I had experienced were enough to make it possible that I was to be the foster father of God's son. Still, I wondered how much of my faith was tied into not wanting to confront Joachim and Anne with accusations about their daughter's own faithfulness to her betrothed, and, even worse, how much of it was tied to not wanting to lose the most beautiful and wealthy young bride in all of Galilee. This wavering between faith and doubt consumed me, in part because I knew what the Most High felt about waverers; hadn't Moses been denied entrance into the Promised Land for one moment of hesitation? What punishment might await me if I continued to hold on to reservations? There seemed no protection from danger at either end of my beliefs. But then soon I would be with Mary and I hoped our union would help to dispel all my remaining doubts.

I didn't know exactly what to expect on our wedding night. I was myself a virgin, a strict follower of our law and I confess I was nervous, though anxious for us to start a life together as one. When I entered our sleeping room, the room I had designed, with its light blue walls, its windows with their curtains drawn, I saw Mary sitting on the bed I had constructed for us. She was still fully clothed. I assumed this was part of her gift to me, that she would let me slowly and happily unwrap the secrets of her feminine self before my anxious eyes. When I sat down next to her, though, I sensed her unease.

"Don't worry, Mary. We can go as slowly as you like. After all, we have a lifetime of loving awaiting us and there is no one in the world I'd rather wait for."

"Joseph, my husband, my beloved, I don't know exactly what to say. I should have spoken sooner, but I haven't had a chance to be alone with you since we talked about our blessed child who even now grows in my womb."

Mary still didn't look a bit pregnant; though I knew it was too soon in any pregnancy for her to show. I thought perhaps she was worried about the appropriateness of our coming together now, so I held her hand as I said: "I know the law and there is no prohibition against a pregnant woman being with her husband. So long as she is not discomfited it is lawful, even recommended that the couple continue to share their love for each other."

Mary did not pull her hand away, but her blue-grey eyes seemed to withdraw from me, even as she said: "Yes, Joseph, you know the law well, as Emmanuel's father on earth should. You know then that the prophet says, 'The virgin will conceive and give birth to a Son.' I'm so sorry, my husband, my beloved, but I must remain a virgin at least until the Holy Child's birth."

I let go of Mary's hand, stunned, as if struck by lightning and she took the opportunity to rise from the bed and walk towards the window. "To avoid temptation, I think it best I sleep on your old mat, in the other room; you can enjoy the comforts of this fine bed you have made."

"I made the bed for us!" I responded. "Surely, it's enough for me to be willing to accept a child that isn't mine and believe the impossible is possible; surely, you aren't telling me we cannot become truly man and wife."

"I'm sorry, so sorry," Mary said gently "but this is how it has to be."

"And if I refuse? You know I am your husband now. You have come to my house. Tomorrow morning the seven days of feasting are to begin with me proudly displaying the sheet to demonstrate what we have begun together here. It's one thing to keep private this crazy thing you've asked me to believe, but I won't be shamed in front of the entire town!"

With that shout I rushed up to Mary, grabbed her by the waist and was certain I was about to throw her on the bed she hoped to flee, but her eyes, her beautiful eyes, implored me, and further her words: "You know the law; a wife is always the one who decides if there is to be union. As long as she is not withholding her passion to hurt her spouse, the decision is hers. Please, Joseph, please be one with me in trust; what the Most High is asking of us has to matter more than our feelings."

I looked again in her eyes, and my anger did not go away, but I saw love there, not any desire to hurt; I saw innocence and pleading and unwavering faith in the Most High. I let her go, I sat on the bed, but as she began to leave, I stopped her.

"There is no way the most beautiful woman in Nazareth can sleep on a mat for her wedding night. Please take this bed as my first of many gifts to you. I'm used to my mat. I'll see you in the morning, my love."

Mary rushed into my arms, hugged me, pressed her head against my chest. I withdrew knowing that touch, that embrace I had been longing for the entire year of our betrothal could not go farther without me losing all control. "I'll see you in the morning," I repeated as I went to find my old, dusty mat.

***

Do I even need to say I spent a restless night? What was I going to do when the sun started its ascent back into morning? Jude would be the one to knock on our door. I was supposed to then show him the bed sheet with the mark of Mary's gift of her virginity to me and then he would show the awaiting townsfolk and there would be a shout, the music would play and the first day of a seven-day long feast, carefully orchestrated and controlled by my new in-laws was to begin. What was I going to say to Jude? To the town? To my in-laws? But worry alone never solved a problem and no visiting angel came forth to save me from my impending shame. And Jude arrived inevitably and on time and knocked on my unprotecting door.

"Congratulations and the blessings of the Most High be on you and your bride and all your future descendants," Jude greeted me more floridly than his usual plain speech would have predicted. I guess he thought one had to say something special at this special moment, he little knowing how much I needed any sort of blessings I could encounter.

"Come in, come in," I told him as I practically dragged him into the house.

"What's the matter? Isn't your bride ready to greet the world? Did you keep her up all night with your, with, well, you know," he said, blushing a little. "She can take another moment or two, but the people are beginning to get impatient. As it is I've come an hour later than most of them wanted me to."

I just stared at him, tried to speak a few times but only a bit of incoherent mumbling followed.

"What's wrong with you, man? Get ahold of yourself. Go get the sheet and let's get on with the feasting," he told me with the predictable slap on the back.

"There, there isn't any sheet," I stuttered and then looked down to the floor.

"Of course there's a sheet. What are you babbling about, Joe?" For the first time Jude seemed to catch on that something was terribly wrong. He looked at me, at my empty hands, and repeated. "Of course, there's a sheet, man. Wake your little lamb up and fetch it."

"Of course there's a sheet," I repeated his words. "But there's no blood on it."

I thought this confession would undo me; even though I trusted Jude, what could he do to get me out of this mess?

Jude looked at me, peered into my eyes and then the most amazing thing happened. He started to laugh.

"Is that all, brother?" he laughed some more. "You had me worried there; I thought maybe your bride had fled back to her parents. Don't you know how ordinary it is for there to be no blood?"

"Ordinary? How can it be ordinary?" I wondered. Did scores of young maidens refuse to lie with their new spouses and plead the need to continue their virginity till their sons were born? And why was Jude continuing to laugh?

"Listen, a woman can lose her hymen any number of ways. Most often it's from riding too far on a donkey or camel. Every year that long trip to Jerusalem for Passover and you know Joachim would never have his precious child walk that far. She probably lost hers years ago. It's not a big deal. Happens all the time."

"Happens all the time," I repeated, dumbly. "Happens all the time," I repeated, as if trying to believe it. "But I've been to many a wedding feast. It always starts with blood."

"Chicken blood, maybe, or goat half the time. People don't want their ceremonies diddled with. But, here, I'll go you one better. Go get the sheet."

I followed his command like a Roman soldier afraid of his centurion. I thought first to get the actual sheet from the bed, but I didn't want Mary to know what I was up to, since she would certainly not want to be part of any deception. Happily, her mother had given us several sets of sheets as part of Mary's dowry, so I just grabbed one of them from the small closet in the hallway and ran back to where Jude was waiting.

"What do you propose we do with this?" I asked Jude, as if he were some kind of magician and I his curious assistant.

He withdrew a needle, one used to mend clothing, which he probably always carried in his garment out of habit. He pricked himself lightly on the finger; a bit of blood dripped out – he let it fall on to the sheet, then smeared it to try to make it look less fresh, I suppose. Not ten minutes later the three of us were outside and the music and merriment were fully in swing. A seven-day period of feasting, singing, dancing and tolerating slightly off-color jokes began, with me drinking too much each evening so as to be less concerned about my continuing bachelor's sleep on my old mat, while my bride stayed as virginal as she was beautiful in the bed and bedroom I had fashioned for her myself.

Chapter Four

Not two days after the wedding feast was concluded, and my first day back trying to catch up with all the work I had let go at my shop, Mary reminded me of her plan to visit her cousin Elizabeth to help her with the last stages of her pregnancy and then to stay and help her in her first weeks as a new mother. Of course, the only word anyone had received about this pregnancy was from the same angel who had informed Mary she was to be the mother of the Messiah. I tried dropping hints with Anne and even Joachim, but it was clear that neither of them had heard anything about it. They had no objections, though, to Mary visiting Elizabeth, since they knew she was Mary's favorite cousin, more like an aunt because of the age difference, and they had no idea that Mary herself was with child. Since the trip to Ain Karim was a several days journey, though, they fully supported the idea that I should accompany Mary, leave her off with her relatives then a few months later make the round trip again to fetch her back home. Neither Mary nor her parents seemed a bit worried about me leaving my shop for a week or more at a time twice in two months after having just been shut down for the wedding: whatever Mary wanted seemed like a fine idea to them. How embarrassing it was going to be to get there and find pushing-fifty Elizabeth not with child at all, only added to the madness. But I wasn't going to let Mary travel there by herself or in some small caravan of strangers. I figured maybe if this all were just her illusion after all, seeing Elizabeth as barren as ever might just be the cure we all needed.

Of course Joachim in his wealth was well able to afford a camel for Mary to ride, and you can go a long way in a day on one of them, but unfortunately he wasn't willing to spring for two beasts, so I had to walk alongside and that limited us to less than half the distance the camel could otherwise have covered, thereby making the trip take a full week to complete. Mary almost begged me a few times to take a turn riding the camel while she walked, but I was not going to subject my maybe-pregnant bride to many hours of walking in summer heat. I just couldn't really get angry with Mary, though. Her offers to let me take my turn on the camel were completely sincere, and it plainly wasn't her fault she believed her barren cousin was with child or that she herself was carrying God's son. That was either the Holy Spirit or complete madness at work, neither within her control; I figured we were on our way to figuring out which once we got to Ain Karim.

Seven days walking beside a camel, even a normal, non-angelic one, is no holiday, of course. The stupid fellow tried to bite me more than once, (only me, never Mary) kept independently deciding when he needed a rest, and got spooked at the sound of any wild animal, no matter how distant. Then there was the periodic complaining he did. Camels make a noise somewhere between a donkey's bray and the grunt of an angry old man. This one wasn't shy. And he seemed most happy to sound off whenever I finally was getting to sleep at night in our tent. Still, overall, the trip was uneventful; we had no close encounters with any dangerous animals, never spotting a lion or leopard and only once seeing a small pack of jackals from a distance. I was happy also to miss seeing any two-legged jackals, the thieves that are a threat to any caravan, much less two people traveling alone. Perhaps it was clear we had nothing much they could steal, beyond a small tent, some clothing and our meager food: dried fruit, some nuts, hard bread, things that wouldn't spoil during our long trek in the heat.

The nights of course were cold and our tent was small, but Mary still insisted we keep our distance.

"Okay, I understand you want to remain a virgin to fulfill the scripture, but does it say anything in Isaiah about a woman not being able even to cuddle for warmth with her lawful husband?" I asked.

"Joseph, you have to understand. It's natural for you to have a desire for me, but it's a desire I can't reciprocate now and I don't want to encourage you only to frustrate you"

"Of course, it's not as if I'm frustrated now, sitting in a corner of a tent by myself with the wind whipping against my back."

"I'm sorry, my husband. I'm only trying to do what I feel is right, where the Most High is telling me I should go."

"Yeah, yeah, I know. You always try to do what's right. Yes, I now know only too well," I responded as I turned my back to her and tried to embrace myself against the cruel winds of my early married life. "Yes, you always do the right thing, Mary," I muttered to myself. "And that's most frustrating of all."

We arrived at the home of Elizabeth and her husband, Zechariah, who I knew
was one of the high priests who served at the temple in nearby Jerusalem. Elizabeth
came to the door, almost as if she knew we were arriving, though the camel for
once had kept quiet. Even from some distance I could see that Elizabeth was large
with child.

And when Mary first entered the threshold of the home, and said hello, Elizabeth, normally a very even-keeled and sensible woman, didn't say hello or ask us
about our trip, but instead launched immediately, in a loud voice, into this most
unusual greeting: "Blessed are you among women, and blessed is the child you will
bear! But why am I so favored that the mother of my Lord should come to me? As
soon as the sound of your greeting reached my ears, the baby in my womb leapt
for joy. Blessed is she who has believed that the Lord would fulfill his promises to
her."

Now, I have to admit, the sight of Elizabeth being obviously well on her way
to having a baby should have knocked all my doubts completely away. Who had
ever heard before of a woman not far from fifty years old, who had been married
the past thirty years and considered barren suddenly being able to be great with
child? Still, she seemed to make too much of the child kicking her – hadn't I always
been told, and observed even, that babies in the womb "leap for joy" any number
of times each day, without any holy provocations necessary? Still, if I thought Elizabeth's greeting unusual, what followed out of my young wife's mouth took unusual by surprise:

"My soul glorifies the Lord and my spirit rejoices in God my Savior, for he has
been mindful of the humble state of his servant. From now on all generations shall
call me blessed, for the Mighty One has done great things for me – holy is his
name. His mercy extends to those who fear him, from generation to generation.
He has performed mighty deeds with his arm; he has scattered those who are proud
in their inmost thoughts. He has brought down rulers from their thrones but has
lifted up the humble. He has filled the hungry with good things but has sent the
rich away empty. He has helped his servant Israel, remembering to be merciful to
Abraham and his descendants forever, just as he promised our ancestors."

The two cousins then embraced and I saw tears in both their eyes – tears of
happiness, of rapture almost: what else could account for these strange words? My
wife was to be called blessed by all generations? My bride could herself speak as

eloquently as one of the prophets? And her cousin, who really was pregnant, knew not only that Mary, who wasn't showing a bit, was also pregnant but with no other child than the Messiah himself? I was stunned and walked over to Zechariah, expecting his florid, prophetic speech to come next; after all, he was the high priest in our quartet. Instead he kept strangely silent, even after I asked him what he thought of all of this. I asked again, he stayed mute, and then Elizabeth disentangled herself from Mary long enough to say: "He has been struck mute, for his wavering and disbelief. The Angel Gabriel himself came to announce we would be blessed with a son, and should name him John and that our son would be the harbinger of the Lord himself. All this I know from what my doubting husband has written for me on his tablet."

The Angel Gabriel strikes again, I could not resist thinking and also wondering why everyone but I rated Gabriel in all his awesome radiance rather than the disheveled Shlomo who visited me. Zechariah, with a rueful look, picked up his tablet and scribbled a few words on it and then handed it to me, with maybe half a hint of a smile: "Better just to believe," he'd written, and in that room of believers, I knew there was no longer any way to resist.

Chapter Five

Mary stayed with her cousin Elizabeth for close to three months. Elizabeth gave birth to a healthy, perfectly normal son, who they named John, and Mary informed me later that when Zechariah was asked during the circumcision what the boy would be named he wrote on his tablet, "His name is John," and when the people asked if there were maybe some mistake, since the name was not in his family, his voice was at once restored to him as he said out loud, for all to hear, "His name is John!" I hear he was pretty happy about how it all worked out, even singing and dancing for joy, and you'd have to see old Zechariah to know how funny a picture that had to be. The stubborn old man had learned his lesson well; there was no future in disagreeing with any angel of the Most High.

Being a reasonable sort myself, I determined to try to follow the path my angel had laid out for me. It was easy, of course, during my months alone, again to question what madness I had involved myself in, but work kept me busy and my in-laws were fairly kind to me, so long as I was ready to do whatever they thought best. (I twice rearranged the furniture in my new house to satisfy their sense of what worked best). And when it was time to collect my bride from her cousin's household, at least I got to ride the camel all the way back to Ain Karim, though before departure I had to keep reassuring Joachim that it would be just Mary's ride all the way back.

Mary was showing when we returned, but not enough to make anyone suspicious about the start date for her pregnancy. Her parents were so happy, with Joachim especially anxious for his grandson to come into the world (he was so sure it was going to be a boy, without even any angelic affirmation; it almost made me wish the Messiah could be a woman – why was that any harder to believe than a pregnant wife who had known no man?). Everything in our new life together for the first several months seemed to be going as well as it could. Of course, whenever a Jew thinks things are going well, he's sure to get a surprise: ask Noah, or Jonah or especially Job. And we didn't have far to look, since, after all, we had the Romans.

The news spread like a plague of locusts. The Romans decided, for a reason only their false gods could fathom, that there would be a great census of all the people under the rule of those tyrants, and that every one of us Jews was to be included. If that weren't annoying enough, every man had to go back to the place of his birth to be registered. For me, this of course meant Bethlehem, a journey just as long as the round trip I had just completed to Ain Karim. It seemed senseless, this census, and I also wondered if even the Romans could keep track of things so completely that they'd really come hunting me down if I didn't make the trek. Of course, my having a pregnant wife would not have made any difference to them; I didn't even ask, but I still spoke up one evening during dinner at my in-laws, about whether it wouldn't be better to stay home. For once, Joachim was on my side, as if he were my own father.

"Yes, it's ridiculous even to consider such a journey. This time of year especially, in the early spring, when the weather, especially in the hill country, can be treacherous and when so many other people will have to be traveling, which will certainly add to the number of thieves and villains waiting to waylay them, it would be really crazy to risk it."

"But, father, it has been ordained," Mary responded.

"Nonsense. You two will stay in Nazareth; I'm sure no Roman will seek to harm you for being prudent," Joachim decreed and he next picked up his goblet of wine and raised it, almost as if were sealing his decision with a toast.

"This cannot be, Father," Mary spoke up again, though still in her usual quiet but certain way.

"And why not, my daughter?" Anne asked, with genuine puzzlement.

"Joseph is from the house of David, from the town of Bethlehem. He cannot register in Nazareth."

"I know where your husband was born," Joachim chided. "Leave this decision to the men, my child."

"It is not by the will of the Romans but of the Most High that we must make this journey," Mary said, but she offered no explanation as to why.

"That can't be so," Joachim argued. "Why would the Most High wish for my daughter, many months with child, to brave this trip just to please some pagans?

If you insist that your husband, as a safeguard, I suppose, go and register in Bethlehem, there's no reason you can't stay with us here until his return. You certainly weren't born in Bethlehem."

"Households must register together, father," Mary explained.

"It can't be the Lord's will, perhaps you are mistaken this time, daughter," Anne hoped against hope, tears beginning to fill her eyes.

All of her life, though, Mary had been explaining the Lord's will and her parents had always acquiesced. I knew my own marriage to her was only because of her parents believing that Mary had some mystic pipeline to what the Most High expected. And since we all knew Mary, just like an angel, was incapable of lying about anything, much less what the Lord had inspired her to say, Anne never really had a chance. Joachim looked like he was about to explode, but instead of yelling or demanding that his daughter obey him, he tried to calm himself and said nothing more.

"Joseph, my husband, we must journey to Bethlehem together, as a family," Mary concluded and that ended the discussion.

That night we slept at the home of her parents. Joachim would not allow his pregnant daughter to have to journey at night back to our own home, though I would have much preferred it. At their home we slept in the same bed, which made it all the more painful not to be able to touch my bride. I longed for the birth of the child in good part since it would mean an end to my remaining a virgin husband. I asked Mary when we were alone, why she so wanted another long trip, many months pregnant, back through the hills to Bethlehem. Her words were not her own, but from the book of Micah: "O Bethlehem, Ephrathah, who are small among the clans of Judah, from you shall come forth one who is to be ruler in Israel, whose origins are of old from the days of eternity." The woman knew her sacred scripture. For some reason, she still hadn't shared with her parents the news of the most holy birth to come. Maybe the Most High knew that Joachim and Anne would not have been able to contain themselves, knowing they were to be the Messiah's grandparents. Whatever the reason, Mary and I kept that knowledge to ourselves alone. And whatever the reason, we were going to have to register in Bethlehem and apparently have a baby born, in only the Lord knew what circumstances, in a place far from our home.

***

For our trip to Ain Karin we had taken what is called the "trade route," which goes through lots of hills and passes through Samaria; it's a little shorter in terms of distance, but a more athletic trek. With my wife very pregnant (we didn't know exactly how pregnant, since the Holy Spirit is a very subtle lover), I thought it best to travel the river route instead, taking us from the Jezreel Valley to that of the Jordan River, before the trek up from Jericho to the hills of Jerusalem, just a few miles north of Bethlehem. Mary agreed that less time in the steep hills made sense, and the weather in the valley might also be a little milder. With all the craziness of so many people needing to travel (it seemed like hardly anyone in our town had actually been born there – Joachim and Anne themselves were from Sepphoris and would have to make that short trek there to be registered) Joachim could not procure us a camel; really, he had waited too long to try, assuming that we would not need to go. We had to settle instead for a donkey, but I was grateful that Mary would thereby not have to walk the entire way. We hoped to join a caravan for a good part of the journey, since we were headed towards Jerusalem, but the trip to the little town of Bethlehem we would be making on our own.

The benefit of a caravan of course lies with the idea of safety in numbers; opportunistic highwaymen were sure to be ready to pounce on any of the many people who all now had to travel at once, like crocodiles waiting in ambush for prey who had to come to the river to drink.

But not all crocodiles reside in the same river, and not all thieves await in ambush only.

One of our neighbors, someone who hated my father in law for having beated him in more than one business deal, had put himself somehow in charge of the caravan headed towards Jerusalem. This man owned a small herd of camels and, as everyone knows, camels can cover much more ground in a day than our little, light-grey donkey could manage. (Mary had decided to name the beast Sarah, even though I was pretty sure he was a gelded male.) This camel king also was renting tents and other supplies to people who needed them, so no one was in a position to argue with him No one stood up for us, then, when he refused to let us join his group.

"That miserable beast of yours, the best Joachim could do for his only child and in such a state? I'm sorry, but I can't put so many others to discomfort and days of added travel just so you can try to keep up with my camels."

"And of course," I responded, "the faster you get to Jerusalem, the faster you can get back, to overcharge the next band of travelers."

"Insults cost a man nothing, craftsman, but without a camel, you'll not travel with us."

And so it was that Mary and I had to travel all the way to Bethlehem by ourselves, with only a skinny grey donkey to accompany us. "The Most High will be with us the whole time, protecting his son and the earthly parents he has chosen for him," Mary predicted, with a wan smile.

"Tell that to the wild beasts, the highwaymen, and the high hills near Jerusalem," I muttered to myself.

"What did you say, my husband?" Mary asked.

"We sure could use the help," I answered her with a smile only someone as trusting as Mary could have believed was authentic.

The first few days of the trip we made excellent time, by my estimation more than ten miles per day. The weather was comfortably cool, the donkey cooperative, the nights in our small tent not unreasonably cold. Still, Mary was large with child and no matter how gentle her donkey and flat the valley terrain, it was difficult for her to travel at all, though she never complained. And of course I could not walk but so far each day, particularly since our water supply was to be preciously guarded and our traveling food – flat bread, figs, dates, and nuts not especially sustaining. Even so, being alone with Mary, witnessing her quiet faith and her cherished assurances that all would be well, could not help but make me proud of this woman I had been blessed with.

The third day we had rain. We tried walking through it, but as we traveled it got worse, both the amount of water and the velocity of the wind, so that the footing became treacherous and the donkey uncooperative, no matter how Mary coaxed him. She decided we had to stop, for the beast's sake. This decision was made easier by the appearance of a small cave that seemed, from a distance, to be big enough to shelter the three of us, and upon arrival, not too far off our trail, proved to be so. I feared at first it could be the den of a wild animal, but aside from some sleeping bats, hanging like dark ornaments at the top of the structure, there were no other tenants.

"You see, my husband, how our Lord provides. Just when we need more shelter than our tent could provide, this cave appears, a kind of welcoming miracle." To me of course, a dank, dark enclosure, which needed to be shared with a very wet donkey whose smell combined seamlessly with piles of bat guano hardly seemed welcoming or miraculous. Still, there was no need to badger a pregnant woman with my complaints.

"Yes, Mary. I only hope the Lord of Hosts will continue to provide when we reach Bethlehem. I've had no word from my brother in more than a year now, and can't be certain he will be ready to take us in when we arrive."

"Remember, Joseph, the words of David, the psalm that begins: 'The Lord is my shepherd, I shall not want' and ends, 'Surely goodness and mercy will follow me all the days of my life, and I will dwell in the house of the Lord forever.' Wherever we go, carrying the Son of the Most High with us, we will dwell in the house of the Lord. Like David, we need fear no evil."

Mary was no fool. It wasn't as if she wasn't feeling the discomfort as I was; in fact, she was feeling it far more, all those months along with the Holy Spirit's doings. Still, her faith did not waver. She comforted me; she comforted the donkey; the bats did not molest her as they woke up that night and began their hunts. We rested in more comfort than I imagined possible, though I could not take from my head the delay the rain had caused us, and how much further we still had to travel.

The next two days, as we entered the Jordan River valley, the weather got colder, a bit unusual for the first days of the spring season, but nothing beyond belief. And the cold spurred us on to try to walk faster, so we made good time again. The river was also a good source of water for us, though I worried about the possibility of a crocodile attacking as I filled our water receptacles. I wished I had time to do some fishing, something I have always enjoyed since my boyhood; a fish would have been a nice variant to our meals of bread and dried fruit, but time constraints and my fear of the river crocodiles kept me happy we still had some pistachios.

Of course lions, wolves, bears were not impossible in the region we were traversing. When we camped at night, I kept an ear out for any unusual sounds, including fearful complaints from our Sarah, since I assumed a donkey's hearings and instincts would be more acute than my own. I slept with one eye open, not the best way to rest on a long journey.

It was Mary who first noticed the jackals. When we stopped to rest late afternoon on the sixth day of our journey, she pointed them out to me, only two of them, resting as we were, perhaps thirty yards away. Though they have a reputation for aggression and treachery, they are not known for attacking humans, but I worried they might think of our smallish donkey as a slower antelope and try to take him down. The donkey itself seemed unconcerned, though, so I decided not to worry until, upon our taking up our walk again, the two jackals also got up, and followed at a pace quick enough to keep up with us, but not enough to gain much ground. They seemed content to follow us, and they continued into the night, so that even as I was setting up our tent, I could see them at a distance, watching us. When I pointed this out to Mary, she seemed unconcerned.

"Aren't you worried about having these animals, famous for their cunning, their treachery, following us day and night?"

"They live as God has made them to live," Mary responded. "And remember what it says in Lamentations, 'Even the jackals draw out the breast, they nurse their young ones'. Perhaps this pair is like us, husband and wife; perhaps they too are awaiting a child."

"Let's hope it's not our child they await," I muttered to myself, not willing to try to alarm someone so comfortable in her seeming inability to be alarmed.

The night grew cold. I thought the Jordan Valley was protected from the worst weather by the hills around it, but the howling wind and dropping temperatures had not heard the same reports. It would have been difficult to keep a fire going, and since I had nothing to cook, it hardly seemed worth trying. I thought of huddling for warmth with my wife, but I knew, even under these conditions, that embracing her would kindle my desire like dry tinder to a flame, so I sheltered her as best I could and shivered a distance away from her.

I had been sleeping fitfully all night, but had managed, I think, some hours of sleep, and sensed somehow that dawn was approaching as I drifted off again. Suddenly, I awakened to the sound of our donkey. At first I hoped I was dreaming and did nothing, but the protestations grew louder and Mary awoke too and said: "Something is wrong with Sarah; I had better go and see about it."

"Stay inside, woman," I told her, more gruffly than I intended, but there wasn't any way I would allow her to endanger herself, no matter how protected she thought she was by the Most High. I grabbed my walking staff and approached the lingering darkness. Even as I stepped out, I heard the sounds of animals scurrying away, and heard a kind of happy greeting from Sarah. Then it was I stepped on something a bit warm and certainly furry in the dark. I jumped back startled, but there was no reason for fear. When I reached down to discover what I had stepped upon, I found a large rabbit, newly killed, and then another close by. Just then the first shafts of sunlight appeared in the sky. Mary had edged out of the tent by now and was gently stroking Sarah.

"I must have scared those jackals away from their kill as I came out. What luck – we'll have meat for breakfast – meat to feed that son growing in your belly."

"Praise the Lord, oh my soul," Mary, said, hardly in the way of a direct response. Then she quoted Moses: "He will give you meat to eat in the evening and bread to satisfy you in the morning because he has heard your complaints against him."

What point was there in mentioning that this was meat we would eat in the morning, that we had brought our own bread, which was barley not manna and that these two dead animals were rabbits, not quail? She believed these dead animals were a gift from the Most High; I'm sure she even believed the two jackals were guardian angels that had been sent to deliver breakfast to us, and not just a few unlucky predators scared off a kill. I was too hungry to argue with her. Even the wind had died down, so that my fire was easy to start; its red-yellow flames matching the glory of the rising sun. And we had meat with our bread that beautiful morning. And the jackals were nowhere to be found.

***

A few days more and we approached Jerusalem. Mary had begun to complain about pains that we feared could mean the onset of labor, but prayed were the "false labor" her mother had warned her about. It was odd to hope for something false, but the idea of having our child in a tent, far away still from any possible help, was too scary to consider, though that of course did not stop me from considering it enough to make sleep almost impossible. Of course we now also had to deal with a very different terrain than the Jordan river valley, with hills that were challenging enough under normal circumstances, but really worrisome for someone in charge of a wife heavy with God's child. That little donkey Sarah, though, was surprisingly tough, capable and more patient and cooperative than any of the donkeys of my past experience. And Mary was ever trusting in the Most High's process, whatever it would be. She seemed certain we would have our baby in Bethlehem and the idea of it didn't bother her even a little bit.

We arrived in the town of my birth mid-morning of the eleventh day of our travels. The plan was to get through the census taking, then get to my brother's house before evening. My parents had died years before and my other siblings no longer resided in the little town, but my much older brother Heli had a nice home, and his children were grown and out of the house, so I assumed he could make room for me, though I hadn't had the chance to communicate with him about our visit, since the whole idea of actually going to Bethlehem when Mary was so far along, was not anything I had planned for. Still, my kind, older brother and his wife would surely be glad to see us, and might even find a measure of happiness in witnessing the birth of their new nephew.

The Romans had set up a make-shift census reporting station in Bethlehem's modest market place, in a building usually reserved for the sale of livestock. Many people were lined up outside the building, and I was certain the Romans were having a good laugh over treating us Jews like animals. Thankfully, they intended no imminent slaughter, but they had well-armed, brutal looking soldiers stationed to remind us that they were in command, even in David's city.

The person behind us in line looked familiar; when he noticed me looking at him at first he seemed offended, but then a sparkle of recognition flashed in his bright green eyes and he said:

"Joseph? Joseph, son of Jacob the craftsman? Is it really you?"

"Yes, Saul, it is." I said, as I recognized one of my father's oldest friends. He must have been eighty years old, but there he was, forced to wait in line with the rest of us by these unkind pagans.

"It's wonderful to see you, though too bad it's for such a ridiculous reason, to stand on line here to be counted like sheep," Saul said. He was old, but his eyes were still bright, he stood un-stooped and his hair was long, full and only partially white. "I myself had to journey all the way from Hebron for this nonsense."

"And we from Nazareth," I reported.

"From Nazareth, and with a wife great with child? Why didn't you just stay home?" Saul wondered.

"This is my wife Mary – she felt it was best to obey the law, to not start our new child's life with any potential trouble from these men," I said, pointing to the armed thugs on either side of our line. "Besides, it will be a good opportunity to visit with my brother and his wife."

"Your brother?" Saul shook his head. "I'm afraid you won't be seeing your brother any time soon."

"And why is that?" Mary asked, with maybe a slight hint of concern.

"I hate to have to be the one to tell you, but your brother left yesterday, just hours after he got through this census."

"Left for where? And why?" I asked, already frantic with the thought of having no place to stay.

"Believe it or not, he is headed for Egypt, where he hears they have much need for craftsmen. After Hannah died, he had nothing here to hold him back, nothing but sad memories of better times. Plus his one son is already there."

"My sister-in-law is dead? Why wasn't I informed?" I asked stunned, wondering how much of my sadness was for my brother and how much for myself.

"Who can say? I myself don't live here anymore; I just happened to see him as he was preparing to depart."

To be truthful, my brother and I had never been close, so I wasn't shocked that he would leave the country without sending me word. Still, I had counted on his shelter and on his kind wife's help with childbirth and now we would have no place to stay if the child was ready to be born. Mary was convinced the Most High's progeny had to be born in Bethlehem, but where in this town would that now be?

My distraction over the bad news Saul had delivered left us dawdling on line. The Roman guard didn't care for any disruption of order.

"Get moving, Jew," he scolded me, the "get moving" part in fractured Aramaic, but the "Jew," in Latin, "Iudeaus," one of the only Latin words I knew, since whenever it came from a Roman mouth it sounded more like a curse than the name of my people.

"What's the hurry?" Saul asked, in a friendly way. "A little gap in the line won't cause any problems," he reasoned.

"Silence, Jew," was all the guard responded, with a threatening gesture towards his sheathed sword. Saul and I knew better than to speak back. We moved up to fill in the small gap in the line our conversation had caused.

After similar mistreatment and more than an hour's wait, we finally took our turn with the census taker and were allowed to depart. But where to? I asked Mary as we headed back to where we had tethered Sarah.

"The Most High will provide. Even in this little town of Bethlehem there must be a place or two for travelers."

"I don't even know where to begin to look," I responded, trying to make my voice sound calm, but certain I was failing.

"Well, my husband, we must begin our search; I think the baby might be with us before the night has ended."

This was Mary's gentle way to say she was having pain – labor pain. I had to find a place for her and very soon.

Chapter Six

The cave was really spacious; the goats, the fowl, and the owner's mule all had sufficient room. None of the animals seemed to object to our presence either; in fact we put Sarah in a makeshift stall right next to the mule and neither of them seemed a bit disturbed. The trick was to find room for ourselves and for the little one to come. The owner let us take an old manger and line it with hay and he told us we could settle in wherever we could make room, so long as we didn't disturb his milking goats. That man really was fond of his goats.

That goat affection was the reason he even offered up his stable as a landing spot for us, after telling us there was no room in his actual "inn." To call the place an inn to begin with was being very generous; the man and his wife had a modest three-bedroom home; two of the bedrooms they rented to infrequent boarders. It was our bad luck that both rooms were occupied, by Roman soldiers assigned to Bethlehem for census purposes only; neither pagan was inclined to offer up his bed for a very pregnant Jew or her crazy-frantic husband.

"If it were up to me, I'd have them both out on their ear. I'm lucky if they'll even pay me when they get ready to leave. What recourse will I have if they decide not to? To whom am I going to complain besides God himself, who is very good at keeping silent about these Romans. Sorry, but there's nothing I can do."

The owner, a handsome man, tall, erect, with black hair and a heavy beard, and piercing dark eyes that shone with the indignation he really seemed to be feeling, kept looking at Mary and when she yelped just a little from a sudden pain, his sympathy also seemed real.

"B'sh'ah Tovah," he said to Mary, the blessing for a pregnant woman, but it almost seemed as if he were trying to forestall the "good hour" of our son's birth from coming too soon by invoking that blessing. "I'd give you my own room I really would," he continued, "but, as I've told you, my wife is not well and I can't in all mercy make her leave the comfort of her bedroom, what little comfort it is. If not for that, the two of us would sleep with the goats tonight and let you have the space. But it can't be helped."

"And where do your goats sleep?" Mary asked, with a gentle, kind tone that only a Roman could be immune to.

"Oh, my goats, my beautiful goats – wait till you taste the cheese that comes from them – the best you'll ever have had. Why they sleep in the cave just next to our home. I've fixed it up for them; it's nicer than some houses."

"And do you think your goats could bear some company for a time?" she asked.

"You're not thinking of sleeping in a stable with farm animals?" I asked, indignant enough for her comfort, but wondering how Mary could believe for a minute that the son of the Most High should enter the world in such a place.

"And why not?" the innkeeper asked. "I'm not joking; many people don't have such a nice abode. There are no swine in my stable, no animal that would defile a woman to look upon as she is with child. It's a wonderful idea, young woman. It's no time to be proud. We'll make you comfortable. Let's go."

Mary smiled, thanked the man and looked at me with those eyes, half way between blue and grey that could never be denied anything I might offer. We made our way to the cave.

Of course my plan had been to stay with my brother and to have his wife help with the delivery, since a man is not to look upon his wife when she delivers the child, and I thereby had no sense of how I could help. This fact buffeted me all the more since I had never once seen Mary unclothed. How were we going to get through this? Where was the Lord of Hosts when you needed him?

The innkeeper, whose name was Micah, was as good as his word. He took time to be certain we were as comfortable as possible. I'm sure there are poor people who have less comfortable hovels they must dwell in than the cave where the son of the Most High was to enter the world. Still, it seemed ridiculous to me that the Lord would choose such an unlikely place for his only son. Perhaps it had all been a lie from the start. The only thing that made me doubt that conclusion was my now complete certainty that Mary had known no man, had never been unfaithful to me. Still, it wasn't impossible a demon had tricked her, tricked us, and led us now to this unholy place to have his unholy child instead, perhaps a child who would be part goat, even. I tried to keep such unholy doubts from suffocating me, especially since it is difficult for those who lack faith to pray. And I really needed to pray.

Mary rested in the hay as well as she could. She moaned with pain, but I could see she was trying her best not to alarm me, though I remembered my own mother telling me more than once, that no pain a man could endure could compare to the pain she had suffered to bring me into the world. Still, Mary tried to keep a smile on her face, tried to reassure me. I could see already that my mother had been right also when she told me a woman could bear pain with grace that a man might not survive.

"Nothing can be more natural, my husband. All will go well."

"Are your pains getting closer together? Is there something I should be doing?" I asked.

Mary didn't answer. I could tell she was praying. She didn't look frightened but rather suffused with faith and love. A she-goat came near to her and I was at first ready to ward it off, but it too was gentle as any lamb and almost seemed there to protect my wife. She stood nearby and responded to Mary's moaning with her own soft bleats. I too decided to pray.

The cave was lit only by my one lantern; the innkeeper had been generous in refilling it with oil. Its rays were sufficient, though, for me to see everything I needed to see, my wife in her pain, the gentle goat, the now quickly diminishing time between Mary's contractions. I prayed the Psalms of David I had been told to pray near delivery. I offered to take any pain the Most High would see fit to place upon me if he might only see my wife, my lovely, holy Mary through this crisis. It was then I fully refused to believe in a demon birth. I knew somehow there was only holiness in that dark cave, and I prayed some more.

Suddenly there were voices and the footsteps of people approaching the cave. Micah came in and he was accompanied by a woman.

"Am I too late?" the woman asked, breathlessly, and with real concern. "Am I too late to be of service?"

I looked to our innkeeper and he explained: "This is my wife Ruth. When I told her who I had in the cave she jumped out of her sick bed like someone fleeing a fire. She insisted on coming to see if she could help."

"But if she has a sickness?" I questioned.

"My sickness is mostly of the heart," Ruth explained. "Micah and I have not been blessed with children, though I have longed for a family for as long as I can remember. I will do your child, your spouse only good. And I have much experience; I am the oldest of nine children; I have experience no man can have."

"You are a blessing from the Most High himself, Ruth," Mary said, with a voice closer to that of an angel than to a woman suffering in such pain.

"Prepare a place for your child," Ruth told me. "Micah, warm water to bathe the child after he is received into the world. And pray, always pray."

Ruth was a short, frail woman but her kind nature seemed to give her strength; I felt certain she and her husband were gifts to us from the Holy Spirit. My confidence and happiness grew, even as I heard Mary cry out, again and again, since I could also hear Ruth's words of encouragement, her confident voice telling me that all was proceeding in a normal way. It seemed to take forever, but soon I heard a loud, lusty cry, and then more crying still, the loud, indignant but certain cries of a newborn baby. I went down on my knees to praise the Lord, to thank the Holy Spirit, to bless the day the Lord had chosen me to stand in for him as father to this infant boy. Micah had returned with the water; after the baby was made clean, these wondrous strangers put him in swaddling clothes, perhaps the very clothing they had hoped to place on their own child, and Ruth handed the child to me. When I held him and gently swayed him in my arms, he soon stopped crying, and looked up to me as if he knew me. I looked for some sign that this child was the actual son of the Most High, but I saw instead a newborn infant, seemingly as helpless as any human infant, and so one who would need me to love and protect him for years to come. And the pride I felt just in holding him in my arms and settling him away from his cries, made me know I would do anything to make him safe and secure. I walked him back towards Mary, but Ruth said, "No, you hold him for now; the after birth is still to come and I must administer to your wife. Then you can be together in your joy."

"Congratulations and a million blessings upon you," Micah said to me as he peered at our little child. "What name will you give this son of yours?"

"His name shall be Jesus," Mary called out, in a voice triumphant with the glory only a new mother can know.

"Jesus," I repeated. "And may the blessings you wish upon us, return to you and your wife a million-fold," I said to Micah.

"Amen," Mary, said. "Amen," she repeated, and even from a distance, and with my vision partially blocked by the she-goat who had never strayed far from my spouse, I knew her eyes were radiant with thankfulness and joy.

Chapter Seven

Once Ruth was finished taking care of Mary, who she said came through the birth without complications, I encouraged my wife to rest, but was not surprised that she was wide awake with excitement and joy. The baby continued to cry but, with Ruth's directions, Mary began to suckle and soothe the child. On Micah's invitation I went back to his house with him so that we could then return to the cave with food – two kinds of bread, dried fruit, and of course goat's cheese.

"I wasn't anticipating these expenses, expecting to stay with my brother only to find he no longer lives in Bethlehem. I don't know how I will be able to pay you."

"Don't worry about it," Micah said as he patted me on the shoulder before picking up his share of the food to be carried. "You're sleeping in a cave, not my good room, and the man who doesn't provide for a family who has just given birth is no man at all. Besides, you look like a strong working man; your wife must not travel for some days still; perhaps you can repay me by helping me with some projects around this place."

"I'm a skilled craftsman, if I may be honest. I'll do whatever you need to have done by way of my craft or any more humble service. Your kindness to us I can never really repay."

"I could tell when I first saw you that you were good people, so your thanks is the only payment needed for now. Let's get this food to the women."

Not long after we had something to eat, Ruth and Micah left us, with instructions to come to them, no matter the hour, if there was anything the new mother and her child needed. We thanked them again for their kindness and tried to settle in for the night. The baby gave no indications, no signs of being the son of the Most High; he cried like a newborn infant cries, he sought his mother's breast, like any baby would, he made water and needed to be cleaned up, like any helpless child. Of course, he also made a good night's sleep impossible, no matter how fatigued we were, but after a time I was actually asleep, in the early morning hours before dawn, but was awakened, not by the cries of the child this time, but by a strange music and singing that seemed to grow louder as I awoke more completely. Soon it seemed as if the strange sounds were coming right from the entrance to the cave. There were tambourines keeping rhythm, rustic flutes playing a steady, stately melody and multiple voices singing: "Glory, Glory to the Most High. All praise the new born king." There followed verses that were harder to make out, but the refrain was clear: "Glory, glory to the Most High; All praise the new born King."

Mary of course awoke too as did the child: who could stay asleep with that joyous racket? "I told you we should have taken Ruth's offer to move into the house with them. Now who knows what awaits us?" I said to my wife.

"And I told you, my husband, that this is where we must remain for now. And the reason why is in the very songs of joy you hear."

I took my lantern and clumsily attempted to light it in the dark, though as I walked with it closer to the cave's entrance, the light from the lanterns of the madmen outside made my task much easier. As I came out to see who they might be, Micah arrived, with a lantern of his own, looking at least as groggy and upset as I myself must have looked.

I counted seven men, shepherds, clearly, both from their manner of dress and the unmistakable fact that they were surrounded by sheep.

"Shepherds, why this jubilee?" Micah asked in an angry voice. "Don't I pay you to guard my flocks? What are you doing out this hour of the morning with them? And why the dancing and singing and merriment? Are you trying to out howl the wolves?"

At the sound of Micah's voice the men stopped singing and stood there looking more than a little embarrassed, all except for one, a tall, strong looking fellow who proclaimed with a deep, beautiful voice: "Angels we have heard on high."

"On high what?" Micah wanted to know.

"On high nothing – just on high, you know, above us. We were minding our flocks, a good ways from here, before getting them settled in for the night when suddenly we heard a heavenly song. I know it may sound crazy, Cousin Micah, but there were actual angels, they had to be angels, since who else could be on high like that? They told us: 'Go into Bethlehem and see the new born king. Give honor and praise to him.'"

"You've all emptied your wine flasks at once. Do you think I too am a madman to believe all this?"

"I'm telling you the complete truth," the tall man affirmed. "We searched for hours, high and low, and received more than one rude reception, I can tell you, until, Samuel over there, our youngest said – 'Why don't we follow that strange star?'"

"What star was that?" I asked.

"Why it's begun to fade a bit by now, but it's right there over this cave, man, a star larger than any we'd ever seen before and so blue it's almost purple. As we followed it we all were filled with the feeling that we were finally going the right way, so again we broke out in song, as we come in hopes of paying our humble homage to the new born king."

"You're madmen," Micah insisted and he looked like he might soon start tearing at his beard and clothing in frustration. "This is where my fair wages go – the merriment of madmen? Does this look like the court of King Herod? Does this look like a court at all? You all know me, Micah, the innkeeper and goat breeder, the owner of some sheep and other livestock. We have no king here, just this man and his wife, all the way from Nazareth, who are here for the crazy census, and who just were blessed with a baby boy, who lies inside in a manger of all things because the Romans have taken up my only rooms. This here is Joseph the Craftsman, he's no king, no prince awaits you within. Go. Leave before I fire you all. And get these sheep back where they belong."

The shepherds again looked chagrined but their leader less so. "Listen to me, Micah. You know I am a sane and sober man. I'm telling you that angels of the Most High appeared to us and commanded us to rejoice and to pay our respects to the new born king. And you know what happens to people who don't follow the commands of angels."

Before Micah could answer, I responded: "Yes, well I know, my friend, better than you can imagine. I'll look in to my wife and see if you can step in for a moment to see the child."

"Let them enter." I heard Mary's response before I could even get all the way back to the entrance. One by one they came in, followed by some of their curious sheep.

"Wait, my goats won't care for those sheep," Micah cautioned, but they were not to be held back. The awakened goats and other animals were not upset; rather they seemed almost joyful – the baas and bleats we heard were soft and a kind of hymn all their own.

One by one the shepherds came in to see the baby Jesus, who was now fully awake in his mother's arms. All of them said a blessing and smiled at both son and mother and then congratulated me on having such a fine young son. The child did not cry; he looked at them, it seemed, with alert, even perceptive eyes, though I've been told that newborns don't see very well at all. A few of the men gave us humble gifts, a piece of cheese or dried fruit; the youngest, a boy himself, gave us a reed instrument he said he had fashioned himself: "Someday the child may make music with it." Micah, looking on, perhaps noting their reverence and something far more mystical than drunken in their comportment, stopped his complaining and told their leader: "Joshua, you have done well. I believe now that you were blessed with a vision of angels from on high. And I see now this may be no ordinary baby. Blessings have come then to my house for offering the small aid my wife and I have managed."

"Your blessings shall be great, even as your kindness to us has proven," Mary proclaimed, as if a prophet. "And blessings to you, shepherds, for you will be remembered always, as will this holy night."

Mary had spoken in this formal, inspired manner frequently for much of her life; some in our town had thought it made her seem strange. Now instead she seemed wise with love and the shepherds bowed to her as they left, once again taking up their flutes and tambourines and lifting their voices in song in honor of this little baby, this new born king of our people.

Chapter Eight

We spent the next few days and nights in the cave, with Ruth constantly apologizing for our setting and begging us to come take her bedroom, while we countered that the cave was comfortable, the animals not a problem, and that we preferred not to stay in the same house as the Roman soldiers, who were capable of who knows what savagery. Mary had had what Ruth defined as a fairly good delivery, but she still of course was weak and sore from the event, and she rested as much as possible. The baby Jesus still showed no signs of being anyone extraordinary.

"Isn't it strange," I said to Mary, "that this little helpless boy, who seems so normal in every way, could actually be both our Messiah and the son of the Most High?"

"Do you still doubt it, my husband, after all the signs we have witnessed together?" Mary asked, but with no judgment in her tone.

"No, there is no doubt left in me. I still can't understand why the Lord would want his son to have such a humble start in life, but I know now more than ever that the Most High is beyond all human understanding."

"Now you're sounding like the man who our Lord has chosen to protect and love his son," Mary nodded.

"I'll try to do whatever is best for the child, and pray it is what God wants," I promised.

"That's all either of us can do," Mary agreed, and she patted my hand as we sat together admiring Jesus, who lay asleep in the manger, innocent of all our worries.

On the fourth day the Romans left, the census time having been completed. Now we happily accepted the offer to move into one of the available rooms in the inn. I insisted on wanting to pay the normal rate, though, honestly, I had not brought along enough money to make that insistence meaningful, but Micah once again brought up the idea of me working for our room and board. The plan was to stay in Bethlehem until it was time to present the child at the Temple in Jerusalem; it made no sense to travel all the way back to Nazareth only to have to make the long round trip once again when the time for the presentation arrived. We had forewarned Mary's parents that if the child were to be born, as Mary had insisted he would be, in Bethlehem, we would stay with my brother until it was time to present the child. It made sense, then, since I had no brother in Bethlehem to take Micah's offer and work for him until it was time to take our first-born son and get him consecrated to the Most High. My decision made Micah very happy.

"You know, Ruth and I have done very well with this place – it has a good reputation – do you know those Romans actually paid their bill, and with praise for Ruth's cooking and cleanliness? I guess even pagans can't deny when they find something good. My idea is to make some additions to the house and then let the whole building be for lodgers, but besides those additions, I'd need to build a small, snug place on that lot nearby for us to live in. So you can see I need a skilled craftsman like yourself – it's as if the Lord himself sent you here to help me. With Mary in our home now where Ruth can be with her, I hope you'll be able to give me a full day's work soon."

I readily agreed and so we set to work, with some additional hired help, to build a small but solid new home for Micah and Ruth, so that they could live in it before any new construction was done on their present home. I enjoyed being in charge of such a project and giving something back to Micah and his wife for all their kindness to us. Ruth seemed like a new woman having a baby in her house; she no longer seemed ill at all and claimed instead that she had never felt stronger.

A local rabbi performed the circumcision, on the eighth day, according to our law. After he completed the ceremony, right there in Micah's inn, we had a small celebration. Mary chided our friends for their extravagance; they slaughtered a lamb for the occasion; Mary also regretted that her parents could not be present.

"They'll have plenty of opportunity to spoil the child once we return to Nazareth," I told her. She smiled, but I could tell she still felt her parents' worry and pain.

When we had completed all the rites of purification according to Mosaic law we took our baby to Jerusalem, the only place where he could be properly consecrated to the Lord. Micah suggested we take another of his lambs to offer as a sacrifice, but Mary insisted it would not be necessary, though certainly Joachim and Anne would have approved. Instead we purchased a pair of doves, right in the market in one of the temple courtyards, trusting that the Most High would not be offended and that we were still following the law.

It was in another of the courtyards outside the Temple proper that we made our offering; of course no one but the High Priest could enter inside the temple proper, the Holy of Holies. Even as the temple building was larger than anything else in all of Judea, so too were the courtyards spacious and usually full of people. It took us some time to find our way to the proper place. Right after we had offered the doves and just before the presentation of our child, a very elderly man came up to us. He looked at us with benign brown eyes that shone brightly in spite of his wrinkled skin and crooked posture; his flowing but neat white beard made him look most wise. He asked if he could hold the baby. I hesitated, but Mary gave the child to him readily, as if she knew him. He held our baby and soon after cried out: "Lord of hosts, now you can dismiss me your servant in peace. For my eyes are seeing the salvation which you have prepared in the sight of all, a light for revelation even to the Gentiles and for the glory of your people Israel."

Though I had heard the words of Elizabeth, though we had been visited by angels, though humble shepherds had proclaimed our infant child a king, I was still amazed by what this stranger said to us, and I could see Mary too was impressed. Still, because of all the signs I had already witnessed, instead of thinking the man crazy, I instead listened with respect and awe to his explanation to us.

"My name is Simeon. I have lived on past the point of a normal lifetime, knowing I would not perish until I had seen the Lord's Christ. This was promised to me by the Holy Spirit and has been fulfilled this very moment."

"Simeon, one so taken with the Holy Spirit, would you give us your blessing?" Mary requested.

He blessed us and the child and all seemed well, but then he added, "This child is destined to cause the falling and rising of many in Judea, and to be a sign that many will speak against, so that the thoughts of many hearts will be revealed." He then looked particularly to Mary, while he handed her son back to her and said: "And a sword will pierce your own soul as well."

"What's that supposed to mean?" I asked in wonderment, but Simeon had already turned and begun to walk away; I wanted to follow him and ask him what he meant by scaring a new mother with such a prediction, but Mary held me back telling me it would be "disrespectful" to follow the old man or seek to question his words. Still, we continued towards the actual presentation with renewed worry and, on my part at least, even fear. Why would a child destined to be the Messiah, the Savior of his people, not be a complete source of joy and pride for his parents? Had anyone ever withstood the power and magnificence of the Most High? What sword would the Lord allow to pierce the very soul of the mother of our Messiah, the Lord's son?

The presentation completed, we began to leave the courtyards, when an even more elderly person, this time a woman, whose clothing was clean but very worn and who seemed almost too frail to walk, found her way over to us. She too was a prophetess. She explained to us that she had lived all her life since her widowhood many years before in the temple grounds, devoting herself to prayer day and night and to constant fasting. She too blessed our child, she too told us her life had been fulfilled in this moment of holding her savior; she too gave us a blessing. Though her benediction did not end with a dire warning, I somehow sensed that she also had something more to say. After taking a few moments more just to hold our child, who so far seemed content to be held by anyone without giving the slightest protest, this elderly woman Anna added, "And you, Blessed Mother of all Mothers, honored by the Most High unlike any woman ever was or shall be, you, Blessed ever Virgin, take back this child, miracle of our faith; love and protect him and prepare him for the trials that will follow." She then left us to proclaim to all who would listen about the miracle that was our little infant Jesus.

As we made our way out from the temple grounds, I tried not to be too depressed by what I had heard. Mary could tell I was upset. She touched me lightly on my right arm and said:

"It is not for us to judge or know what will come from being the parents of this child, but we know it will end in glory."

"Yes, my wife, I'm sure you're right," I nodded, without conviction. I worried mostly for her sake; it seemed the sword was meant just to pierce her soul and not mine. Still, I vowed that no sword, real or symbolic, would ever come near my wife without first having to pierce me as well.

Chapter Nine

As we arrived at the spot where we had tethered Sarah, who waited patiently for us among all the other tethered animals, I found myself coming back to one particular phrase of the Prophetess Anna. She had called my wife "Blessed Mother of all Mothers" but of course I understood the reason for that designation, since she clearly believed Mary's son to be the Messiah. The part that troubled me was when she added "Blessed ever Virgin," and that phrase I pondered silently to myself for miles as we made our way back to Bethlehem, where I had convinced Mary we needed to remain for at least another week in order to complete the work I had agreed to for Micah and Ruth's new home. What had that old woman, with her dull, filmy eyes that could scarcely see meant by that phrase? Mary had kept herself from contact with me through to the period of her mikveh, but now that she was ritually clean and purified, I assumed we were soon to start a normal married life together. How had Anna possibly known Mary was still a Virgin? After all, she saw her with the child. Had the angel Gabriel also somehow blessed her with this otherwise secret information? And as much as I wanted to twist the phrase around to mean that Mary was just the ever-blessed young woman who had had the miracle of staying a Virgin through childbirth, the more natural meaning of the phrase, that she would forever be both blessed and a Virgin, gnawed at me with its logical insistence. Still, even a Prophetess was no rule maker, no angel sent from the Most High to instruct us. I hesitated, though to bring my worry up to Mary after all we had just been given to worry about by the two elders.

Intimacy would have been difficult for a normal couple, with a baby who woke us up every few hours with his cries and being in the strange surroundings of Micah and Ruth's inn. I decided it made sense not even to bring up the subject again until I had shared with Mary my plan to start our new life in Bethlehem, with some distance from my imposing in laws.

To me the plan made a lot of sense. We would go back to Nazareth to introduce the baby to his grandparents, but then I would close up my shop, gather its contents and head back to Bethlehem. Micah had big plans and I already felt closer to him and Ruth than to any of our neighbors in Nazareth, with the exception of my friend Jude. Besides Micah's plans to expand his own place, he also had given some thought towards constructing a much larger inn in Jerusalem itself. He had approached me with the idea of becoming his second in command in all his enterprises; he also pointed out that with my brother's removal to Egypt, there was also a need in Bethlehem for a craftsman to take his place. Though Mary would be upset at my idea, I thought I had some good arguments to help her to agree. As a highly observant Jew, Mary would want to travel to Jerusalem each of the three times yearly that it was necessary to do so. How much easier would those journeys be from nearby Bethlehem than from distant Galilee? And since she knew her child was the son of the Most High and destined to be our Redeemer, wouldn't it make more sense to raise him close to the Temple in Jerusalem instead of so far from that holy place? Finally, wasn't I the husband, the breadwinner, the man, who, even though unhoused from my role of birth father still should have all the rights of respect and authority the holy books called upon my wife to acknowledge and respect? Though I did not want to upset Mary, I thought perhaps she owed me something too; being the fake father of the Messiah was not going to be easy; it might be a little easier if we could get away from my in-laws.

So it was that the one week more I had promised to Mary extended to a month and then longer. Each time I put her off, saying that my work was essential to the success of Micah's ventures, and that I could not leave him short after all that he and Ruth had done for us. I was surprised that Mary did not object much at all. She simply maintained that what the Most High decreed would come to fruition. No matter how I laid plans against it; Mary was confident that Jesus would end up a Galilean. The knowing looks she would give me drew me close to anger. "It's your son who is the Messiah, not you," I'd remind her. "You don't know everything and he can't talk yet to tell you his wishes."

One day during this time I returned from a short journey for building supplies when I was astounded by the sight of no fewer than nine camels outside Micah and Ruth's home. I saw also men attending to the camels, and perhaps guarding the materials that were laden on a few of them. These men bowed to me as I prepared to enter Micah's inn. They were not of our kind, I could tell by their dress and that none of them responded to my greeting, as if they did not understand our language. When I got inside, I was more astounded still. Mary was surrounded by more strange men, I counted four, three of whom were arrayed like Kings, with flowing robes of purple, red and green and two of them with turbans on their heads. Another man, less royally arrayed and turban-less, much shorter than the others and with a complexion closer to our own, saw me enter and asked, in a raspy but confident voice in our own language:

"Ah, and is this the husband? Shalom, my friend. Your spouse insisted we await you before delivering our gifts. I'm happy to make your acquaintance. I am Levi, once of Bethany, but now a world traveler and guide."

I gave Mary a look to register my surprise, but she seemed calm, as if it were an everyday occurrence to have camel-riding royalty arrive with gifts for her child. That knowing look was getting more exasperating by the minute. Still, the men seemed to mean no harm, so I replied: "Welcome, Levi. Shalom. We are visitors here ourselves; this is not my home but that of our friends Micah and Ruth, so I cannot extend anything more than a greeting to you and your friends."

Levi gave me an exaggerated bow. "My 'friends' as you call them, are Magi, from a distant land that worships not our Most High Lord, yet these men study the ways and customs of all, and they have had us follow a brilliant star to come to this spot to pay homage to a new born king of the Jews. We have been to the very court of Herod the Great, which seemed to me the most logical place to find a new king, but we found no satisfaction there, though Herod received my Lords well, and seemed very interested in our pursuit. It has taken us this long to find this humble spot, but my Lords insist our journey has ended and your son is the king they have sought."

Levi spoke rapidly, as if he were selling wares in the public market. He seemed almost amused as he shared his news with us. I got the impression that so long as his "Lords" were footing the bill, he'd be happy to believe anything they wanted him to believe. I didn't know quite how to respond to him. Mary, though, had no such problem.

"Tell your 'Magi' that we are much honored by their visit. Now that my husband is here to witness this moment, we would be further honored by introductions and the gifts we are unworthy of, but which we will accept in our child's name."

As she spoke the Magi, (the very word would have struck fear in me, if they had not looked with so much benevolence upon Mary, who held Jesus in her arms as she spoke to them) stepped forward and looked to Levi for introductions.

"May I introduce to you, Larvandad, Gushnasaph and Hormisdas, each of them expert in astrology and the understanding of man's destiny in this world. They haven't much skill in speaking our tongue, but a reading knowledge of Hebrew has them well acquainted with our holy books and it is through them, and their study of the stars that they have arrived on this spot. Each of these wise men, these prophets-priests of their strange religion, has a gift to offer your child."

All three of the Magi were tall men, two of them seemed not much older than me, and like me they had dark beards, though their complexions were shades darker than my own. The third man, who seemed in some sense to be the leader had a flowing white beard and a face marked by the wrinkling of time. It was one of the younger men, Larvandad by name, who stepped up first. As he bowed to give his gift to Mary and me, Levi translated the words he spoke. "I give the gift of gold, finely wrought and worthy of a king." He placed in my hand, a small but heavy replica of a strange animal, with big ears and a long snake-like appendage where its nose should have been. As I looked on in wonder, Levi explained. "They call this beast an elephant; it is larger than anything else that walks the earth; in faraway lands kings and generals ride on them in glory."

We thanked the young man for his gift. He bowed deeply again, stepped back and the next young Magi approached, the one called Gishnasaph: "I give the gift of frankincense, the incense used to make a fragrant pledge of adoration to a god." Levi spoke these words as he translated them. But he himself seemed perplexed and spoke to Gishnasaph, as if he wanted to be sure he had heard him correctly. He turned to me and winked: "Yes, he really seems to think your little son there is some sort of deity. I mean, I figured the king thing was a stretch, but now it's getting a little ridiculous, am I right? Still, that incense he just handed over is practically worth its weight in gold, so you folks are making out pretty well here, so I won't try to talk them out of it." Levi ended his speech with a wink, to let us know he was on our side no matter how silly things got.

Mary did not get offended by Levi's assumptions, and, after all, why wouldn't he think it at least a little crazy for these strangers, who had just come from being well-received at Herod's court, to instead be handing over expensive gifts to a humble family with a very ordinary looking child? The time came, then, for the older man, Hormisdas, to speak.

"I am Hormisdas. I have devoted my life to the study of godly things, the stars, the holy books written by men of wisdom. In our religion we believe there is a constant battle between the Prince of Light and the Prince of Darkness. They have almost equal power, which is why evil so often seems to triumph in this life, but we believe our Prince of Light will prevail. I have come to see this emanation of our Prince, and find him where I least expected to, in his clean but humble house here in the land of Judah. I see great triumph for our Prince, but first great sorrow; thereby I give the gift of myrrh, to recognize his mortality, which he has humbled us by assuming."

"Don't let him scare you – he's always this serious," Levi added. "You can use this myrrh stuff for all kinds of things: it heals sores, the priests use it for their anointing oils – you can sell it for a pretty penny too – these really are great gifts, my friends."

Hormisdas seemed to understand if not the words then at least the tone of Levi's chatter and he looked very seriously towards him, said some other words in his language and indicated he wanted Levi to translate.

"The old gentleman insists I repeat these gifts are for the newborn child, and though he trusts you would never misuse them, he wants to make it clear that they have been given to you in all respect and solemnity. Okay?"

"Yes, of course," I said. "Please pass on our thanks."

"Yes, our deepest appreciation and respect," Mary added, as always not worrying whether it was a woman's place to speak her mind among these wise men or any others.

Levi seemed to pass on our respects, as the men bowed again and I thought I saw Larvandad smile, even.

"Again, since this is not my home, I cannot speak for certain until I consult my friend Micah, who is not far from here, but I'm sure he and Ruth would want us to invite you to dine with us and to stay to rest from your journey."

Levi didn't translate my words but instead said directly back to me. "Don't worry about it, my friend. These guys have food like you wouldn't believe in the caravan, plus servants and the nicest tents I've ever seen. They also told me they didn't want to stay long at all. They were going to head back to Herod's, but one of them had some sort of presentiment and now they're all hot to get going back home by some other route. I can't figure these characters out for a minute, but they pay me well, so I don't ask too many questions, but I'm sure they want to get away quickly."

"Thank you brother Levi," Mary nodded. "But could you please translate to them my husband's words nonetheless."

"Sure, lady, no problem whatsoever." He proceeded to talk again to the Magi, they bowed yet again, and what they said back, Levi assured us was more or less what he had already anticipated, though he added, "But they want you to know how much they appreciate the offer and how honored they are over getting to see your boy."

After that the men withdrew, with more bowing and what seemed like blessings. We thanked them again and again and I escorted them out of the house myself, leaving Mary indoors with Jesus. The servants immediately set to work helping the Magi mount their camels and getting all else ready to go. As I was saying farewell to Levi, he suddenly hit his head violently with his hand, saying, "Hey, buddy, I almost forgot. Let me go clear it with Hormisdas – wait out here a minute."

He ran over first to talk to the elder, seemed to get his assent then ran over to one of the supply camels. A moment later he came back with two blocks or rather wheels that looked like some sort of cheese perhaps. "Hey, Joseph the craftsman, here's one more gift – this for you and your wife, plus you can share it with the landlords. It's the real gold, friend, the best stuff you'll ever eat – it keeps really well too, which is why we brought so much along with us – this one is plain, the other is filled with pistachios – enjoy!"

"What is it?" I asked.

"The call it halvá – I think they make it out of the sesame plant – the seeds, probably. Don't worry, I'm sure it's kosher – nothing forbidden in it. It's a treat – they use honey, I'm pretty sure – all's I know for certain is you've never tasted anything better. You two are a nice couple – the Lords thought you acted just right

— so they're happy to give you one more gift before we head out. Farewell, brother, on to a new adventure."

I said my final goodbye to the Magi and their wise guy translator-guide Levi. I brought the strange treat inside, trusting it would be good, but both Mary and I were amazed at how good, as were our friends when we shared some with them. It was the one sweet and simple surprise of what had been yet another shocking day in our lives since the angel had first told Mary of the real Lord's plans for us. His son, like the boy's mother, stayed mostly calm and slept that night better than ever. I anticipated a restless night, worrying about what all these new portents could mean, but even I could not have anticipated how really strange my night would turn out to be.

Chapter Ten

We stayed up pretty late, talking over with Micah and Ruth the visit of the travel-ing Magi. They insisted on seeing the gifts we had been given; they remarked on the splendor of the caravan, which they had only noticed as it was leaving their home, since both of them had happened to be visiting with a friend on the other side of Bethlehem when the Magi had arrived. It was difficult for them to under-stand why so much fuss was being made over our son, who still seemed as ordinary as ever, though certainly a healthy and well-loved ordinary at that. It was not our place to tell them that the Magi had treated Jesus as a newborn king; it was not our place to reveal he was the son of the Most High; it was not our place to intro-duce our growing infant as the Savior of our people Israel. Unlike most others, I don't think Micah and Ruth would have laughed or been scornful, especially since they were coming to love our child as if he were a part of their own family, but it still was not our place.

"Your son must be destined for great things," Micah said, as he toasted our family with a cup of wine. Just seeing the gifts the Magi had left us was proof enough that he was not alone in thinking Jesus a special child. Ruth, also, was thrilled for us and not a bit jealous.

"I'm so happy," she said, "that you've decided to stay with us, to work with us side by side, as we build something wonderful here in the place of your birth, Joseph, and the destined place of your son's birth as well. A toast to Bethlehem and our future happiness and prosperity here."

Mary smiled graciously but said nothing, nor did she share in the toast. Of course her ready excuse was that she thought that wine was not a good thing for a nursing mother to enjoy. Where she got some of her notions I had no way of knowing, but once she had one, she always stuck to it. She waited until we were alone that night in our room to comment on what Ruth had said.

"Do you think it is fair to our friend for you to mislead her into believing we are staying here for good? You know that I've told you our son must be a Galilean and that at best we can stay only until their house is completed."

"I've been meaning to discuss this idea with you, but I've been waiting for the right moment," I began with less confidence than I had when practicing to myself how this all should go.

"There can be no right moment to present a plan against the will of the Most High. We must return to Nazareth, and soon."

Mary's voice was still calm and not in direct confrontation in tone. Still, wasn't that always her way? She had always gently insisted and her parents and now I always would let her have her way, with the idea that her holiness made disagreement somehow wrong, somehow unholy. But it was time to assert my rights, my legitimate rights, as her husband.

"Mary, isn't it just that you want to return to be near your parents and all that is familiar to you in Nazareth? It's natural, of course, but I see great things for our family here, much more prosperity working with Micah than I could achieve working for myself in Nazareth. Besides, you'll be much closer to your cousin Elizabeth here, and much closer to Jerusalem, where you'll want to travel often for the holy days. This too is where I, your husband, believe we should stay and surely you know you must honor your husband and accept his decisions for the family."

"This is no ordinary family, my husband," she replied, again, with no sign of the rancor that had started to take over my own voice. "Jesus must be of Nazareth; I know it as much as I know the miracle of his birth, and I cannot go against the will of his true heavenly father." Should I have taken that remark as an insult, as a reminder of the charade I'd be asked to live for the rest of my life? Surely, Mary was not capable of an intentional insult of someone she claimed to love, or of anyone, for that matter. Still, I was in no mood in that moment to explain that to myself. It felt like an insult and I received it as such.

"Yes, I'm not his father. Haven't I already suffered enough from that? Are you going to throw it in my face every time I try to assert my own plans, my wishes, my desires? While we're at it – it's certainly time for us to begin living like a true husband and wife. I've waited long enough – if this little sleeping babe cannot be my true son, certainly others can follow since it is holy and blessed for a properly married couple to become as one."

I moved towards my wife, though I didn't place a hand upon her. I knew that the same Jewish law I had just brought up in my support insisted that it was the woman who always could say yes or no to relations with her spouse. By the look in Mary's face, I read a clear and continued no.

"When will this end?" I shouted. "How can you continue to deny me? How can you think that this is right?"

"You're upset, my husband, over so many things. Perhaps this is not the time to go over what must be," Mary said, and her voice was quavering, though not in fear.

"What do you mean, 'must be'? Where are you taking us now?" I asked.

"You heard the words of the prophetess," Mary said. "'Blessed Ever Virgin.' It has been revealed to me that you and I must never be intimate. The Most High demands that I dedicate my life to our son without the normal relations one has with a spouse. I must remain forever without sin to be worthy of the blessing the Most High has placed upon me."

"There is no sin in a woman's love for her husband. There is sin in denying him this way." My voice still mostly registered frustration, but more and more anger was beginning to take over. Mary looked at me with concern, but without fear, knowing I wasn't a man capable of forcing myself on anyone, much less her. Still, my frustrations made me feel less in control of myself than I ever had felt before.

"A woman only sins if she denies her husband to punish him in some way. You know my heart, Joseph; you have to know how sad it makes me feel to deny you, how sad even it makes me feel not to have this part of our lives together. But no one can be intimate without some occasion for lust either on her part or the part of her spouse, so physical intimacy can have no place in my life. The Lord has chosen you even as he has chosen me. He knows you can understand and live the life he is calling you to live."

As she finished her speech she touched me gently on the hand. That touch was too much for me. It signified all the touching, the caresses, the intimacy she was saying we could never share.

"No, this is too much. I am not a eunuch. I'm your husband. I say we are staying in Bethlehem, and I say you must come to your senses and become my real wife, or I'll sue for divorce. What Rabbi would deny me? I mean, this is really too much!"

"Joseph, I know how much this hurts you, but think too of me. Our Lord demands that I be perfect, always without sin. I didn't ask for this, but I must remain the handmaiden of our Lord; I cannot refuse the wishes of the Most High. And you must help me Joseph, and help our child."

"But he isn't my child, is he? And now I know I'll never have a son to call my own if I stay with you. I'm telling you this is more than anyone should be asked to put up with. I'm a man, not an angel. I'm just a normal man; no one can expect me to be perfect. You be the Lord's handmaiden all you want, but this is just not for me!"

With these words I rushed out of the room, leaving Mary in tears. I didn't know where to go next. The other room available in the inn was occupied by a guest; I headed for the cave. I'd sleep besides the animals; I'd sleep where I had been happy the night of Jesus's birth, thinking of all the good things that were still ahead for me in my life with the beautiful Mary. I'd sleep as best I could, away from the woman who wanted me always to remain away.

Of course my sleep was fitful. At first I didn't try to sleep at all, just paced around the cave until I made the goats so nervous I was afraid one of them might try to buck me from behind. I settled myself by checking on Sarah, patting our donkey gently and telling my troubles to him, as if he could understand. Finally, though, I settled myself in some hay, near the empty manger where Jesus had spent his first hours. I knew Jesus was the son of the Most High; I could have no doubts after all the signs, but I still didn't know how I could live the life or should have to live the life that Mary was dictating. How could I live like a eunuch when I was instead a fully healthy man? And why should we move back to Nazareth where my pushy in-laws would intrude so much in our lives and where we'd always be so far from Jerusalem, where Mary would often want to be, and where one would think the son of the Most High should also often wish to be? It just didn't make any sense to me. I tried to sleep but sleep didn't come for hours. And when I finally did get to sleep I soon found myself being gently nudged, and when I didn't respond, nudged a lot more harshly, this time with a foot rather than a hand.

"What is it? Is it time to work already? Is that you, Micah?"

"No, no Joseph the Craftsman, it isn't your good friend, Micah. Rather it's your angry angel Shlomo."

This news got me on my feet quickly. I looked and saw the same disheveled, mole-nosed excuse for a heavenly being that had first started all my trouble. "What do you want?" was all I gave him by way of acknowledgment.

"Well, I've got some big news, but first I've got to tell you, you can't treat the Messiah's mother this way. She's in her room just now asleep after sobbing for hours. You think it's easy on her? Do you think she isn't suffering? What kind of a man are you, to treat the will of your Lord this way? I mean, who do you think you are, a Prince? You're Joseph the Craftsman – solid citizen, lover of the law, that's why you were chosen, but you're no Prince, right?"

"That's right, I'm just a simple man being asked to do, to accept too much. Did I ask to be the Messiah's fake father? Did I ask to have to spend my life without the love of a woman, even though I'm married to one? Did I ask for any of this?"

"No, but you've been called and you'll keep doing the right thing if you know what's good for you. Meanwhile, the big news. Forget about staying in Bethlehem – that's out."

"Why?" I dared to ask this angel. "If I'm to follow orders, can't I at least know why it has to be Nazareth instead of here in Bethlehem, which was where this child had to be born somehow, but not where he can stay?"

"Foolish man, it's neither Bethlehem nor Nazareth for now. It's off to Egypt with you, and in a hurry. In fact, get up right now and get to packing."

"Egypt? Are you an angel or a madman? Why would we go there?"

Shlomo looked at me with those piercing, dark angel eyes of his and shook his head with regret. "It's a terrible reason, the worst. Those Magi, best intentions in the world, better men as pagans than a lot of the chosen people, but they told crazy king Herod about this new king being born in Bethlehem and he isn't having any of it. And since they decided to elude him instead of ratting out Jesus's location, he's going to have every new son in the area killed, and, just to be safe, any male child up to age two. It's a blessing your friends don't have any children. You'll have to get lost quick, and with the census giving you up, even going back to Nazareth wouldn't make you safe from a king. You've got to get somewhere where he isn't in charge, and Egypt is the nearest place for that."

I was in shock over what Shlomo was saying. So many children to perish? How could the birth of the Most High's son lead to such slaughter? As if he could read my mind (and why couldn't he?) Shlomo added.

"It's grim and awful, I know. But it's only the first-time innocents will suffer or die for the Lord's son's sake. He'll cause almost as much misery as joy for a few thousand years to come, in fact. It's just the way it's going to be. But for now, we have to keep him safe. You have to get out of here and quickly!"

"But this can't be," I insisted. "Why won't the Lord strike down this evil king who threatens to harm his own son? Why must we flee? Why does the Most High not even protect his own?" As I said these last words I sought to put my hands upon the Lord's messenger, to shake him out of his smug decrees and into telling me the full truth. Instead, I found myself only grasping a bunch of hay; I found myself still lying down, with no angel, near, just a goat breathing down my neck and looking upset at all my commotion. It had all been a dream. But I knew enough by now not to doubt a syllable of what I had heard.

Mary didn't hesitate for a moment when I told her the angel's message. We got ready as quickly as we could. We had to awaken Micah and Ruth to tell them of our need to flee and to ask them to warn any of their neighbors with small, male children to protect them if they could. They didn't doubt us for a moment; Ruth gave herself over to uncontrollable sobbing and Micah beat his breast. I could see Ruth's sadness encompassed not only the grim slaughter to come, but the loss of the child in her home, the blessed child they had treated with so much kindness.

"Please get word to my family where we have gone," Mary asked of Ruth, as she embraced her. "The Most High will protect you and bless you always for what you have done for us. We'll hope to see you someday, perhaps, after the danger is past."

The baby Jesus, who I was holding in my arms, woke from slumber and began to cry. His wailing was stronger, more insistent than usual. Though nothing in the way of really unusual, I still sensed his cries had more depth and pain than ever before. It seemed to me he was crying for the innocents who would have to die because he lived; he was crying for the suffering he was to cause his own mother, who now was trying to stop her own tears. Perhaps he was crying also for himself, son of the Lord that he was, yet still caught in the tragedy of being a human being in this world of sin and death. And yet he too was just an infant; for him crying was the most natural thing in the world.

Chapter Eleven

Our journey to Egypt was difficult, but the Derech HaYam an ancient and high-traffic road that borders the great sea had no hills or other obstacles to overcome and so we were able to arrive in that foreign land after a few days journey without any unusual hardship. We had enough food—our friends made sure of that—and Sarah held up well, fortified by her time of rest in Bethlehem. The baby stayed healthy and we met with no thieves or dangerous animals. Of course, we didn't need any particular calamity still to feel the trauma of our circumstance, a young couple traveling with hardly any possessions or means to a strange country with a still helpless child to provide for. Mary seemed to remain calm, trusting as always in the Most High's will, but that just left all the worrying to me and, honestly, made me all the more upset because she didn't share in my anxiety. We didn't speak the language of the people of Egypt; I didn't know how I was to find work, I didn't know where we would find a place to live. My own faith in the will of our Lord was not as steadfast as my wife's, since I could not fathom why or how he could allow his son to be in such constant danger and deprivation.

Of course Egypt was also just as much under the rule of Rome as we were, so the Romans were an additional factor to worry about, though oddly this did make Egypt a bit more connected to our homeland than it would otherwise have been. Still, as we tried to settle first in the tiny town of Farma, just east of the great river Nile, I had only Mary's confidence that we would not soon starve or otherwise meet our end. I in particular felt no confidence. "I know this is difficult," Mary tried to commiserate, "but it's just a trial the Lord is asking us to pass, as he has for so many of the prophets and others he has tested over time. Surely, you're convinced Jesus is the son of the Most High. How can you doubt but that all will be well?"

"Sure, I believe this little baby will grow up to be the Messiah. That's almost the easy part now. He's going to come out of this okay. But maybe my only role was being from the house of David, as foretold. Maybe I'm to perish here, in this foreign land, so you and the child can find a more worthy protector."

"Don't be crazy, Joseph. You too were chosen by the Most High. I knew it the first moment I saw you. Don't let your fear undo your faith."

"Yes, that's good advice," I said, "but one can't eat advice, nor feed it to his family."

We lived in our small tent on the outskirts of Farma for weeks; I journeyed into town each day to try to find work, but for the first several days I couldn't find a thing. Trying to communicate was difficult enough, and there were no obvious tasks in need of workers, no crops seemed ready for harvest, no building being erected, so I could not even find work as a farm hand or laborer. The fourth full day was the Sabbath, so I did not seek work at all, but my fortune seemed to change on the fifth day when I bargained for several days' labor helping a merchant I discovered in town who needed some new stalls built for his wares. I imagined the quality of my work would be a language of its own and help spread the word for future assignments; the merchant himself was friendly enough and paid me what seemed a fair wage.

On the third day of my work for the merchant Haser just before I was to quit for the day, several men surrounded me and spoke to me harshly. One especially large man, a virtual Goliath, threatened me by obvious gestures with a large hammer. "What have I done?" I asked them in a language they could not comprehend. The merchant too was being threatened, so I soon figured out without understanding the actual words spoken that they did not appreciate his hiring of a foreigner to do the work they would have otherwise taken on, and appreciated even less the foreigner who had taken the work from them. This interpretation of their language became even more justified when the giant took his hammer not to my head, but to one of the stalls I had just completed, smashing it into an unrecognizable pile of wood with just several blows from his hammer. My first instinct was to try to stop him from destroying my work, but two of the others held me back, one twisting my arm. There were four of them all together and they were ready to do me harm, so I had no choice but to bow and back down like a woman threatened by an unworthy husband. I was relieved when they decided to let me scurry away without a beating, and their laughter served as a bitter escort, taking me forever away from their town.

The next morning we left Farma and headed towards where the merchant had previously indicated to me there were bigger towns and more opportunities for labor. I was fortunate the merchant had paid me a daily wage and I had been able to buy food with it each of the first few days, since I received nothing for my labor that third day of hard work.

For weeks later we lived a similar pattern; I became a kind of migrant worker, and our family remained in a small tent, where I brought back whatever food I could manage, via work only occasionally related to my skills as a craftsman. I did everything from picking dates to sweeping and cleaning for merchants to cleaning the out buildings for a legion of Roman soldiers. We saw the great river Nile and more than once I caught fish there, with a cane pole I fashioned on the spot. We saw the massive triangular structures I later learned were the pyramids, vainglorious resting places for the pagan leaders of Egypt. Mary mostly stayed in the tent with the child, who was somehow managing to grow, even flourish, his mother's milk a magic drink that kept him strong while we lived on the simplest of fare. Mary would try to insist I eat more than my share, since I was the one working long hours, but her very willingness to sacrifice for me ensured that I could never let her. Besides, that mother's milk had to be fueled somehow; there was no manna from heaven. I was so exhausted and so often humiliated by the work I had had to complete, especially when working for the mocking Romans that I really didn't suffer as much from any lack of intimacy with my spouse. Still, not having any solace from a lover's embrace was one more indignity I had to suffer each grueling day.

Our luck turned one afternoon while we were once again on the road, traveling still further from our homeland in the hopes of finding work. With a baby to carry and a donkey to manage our progress was slow, so we weren't surprised when a man traveling the same road caught up to us. He looked to be about thirty years of age, though he was already mostly bald; his beard was full and dark, though, without a touch of grey. He was shorter than me, but I could tell by his vigorous pace and his sun-tanned skin that he was someone used to hard work and to being outdoors. He had no pack animal and was carrying his possessions in a large sack he had slung over his shoulder. When he reached us, he said, in a friendly voice: "Ahlan wa sahlan," which I knew was how Egyptians greeted each other, but I still hadn't mastered the response, so I just nodded and tried to look friendly in return. The next thing he said surprised me, a simple "Shalom?" I was quick to response.

"Shalom also to you. Are you by any chance Jewish?"

"By every chance, brother. How nice to meet a countryman on this lonely road," he smiled. "They call me Aram. And you?"

"I am Joseph, and this is my wife Mary and our infant son Jesus."

"Happy to know you. Blessings upon you," Aram said, and he seemed to get happier by the minute to be speaking with us. "It's a pretty quiet business, traveling alone. Maybe we can travel together a piece? I'm on my way to Cairo, where I hear there is much work, some big project the Romans have begun, a fortress or some such big-time Roman thing. Are you headed that way?"

"I'm headed wherever I can find work. I'm a craftsman by trade. Do you think there would be work for me there?"

"If you're any good, you'll have more work than you can handle. I'm too un-skilled to call myself a craftsman, but I'm a steady hand at any work that requires a strong back. If your wife doesn't object, why don't we head there together?"

. It was wonderful to hear someone speaking our own language. Mary too was happy to have a countryman in this land so foreign to us, especially one who was so friendly and talkative. And so we journeyed to the great city of Cairo together; Aram and I on foot, and Mary on Sarah; I carried Jesus most of the way. The child still always seemed so quiet and happy when I held him and that somehow made me proud. Aram had some knowledge of the language of both the Egyptians and the Romans, as he had lived as a worker in Egypt for many years, so he was able to talk me up as a skilled craftsman when we arrived at the great Fortress of Baby-lon, more like a walled city than a single building. I learned that it had been there for many, many years and was a place where boats on the great river Nile had to stop and pay a fee to pass. The Romans were rebuilding closer to the river itself, to make it easier to gather water, and so there was plenty of work to be done, woodwork, masonry, perhaps even some work with metal, all of which were within my skill set. I was put to work immediately in helping to construct a large brick wall, and I soon had a good report from the foreman on the work, and so steady labor at last.

Mary was happy to learn of my success; soon we were able to move into a kind of temporary housing the Romans had erected, nothing as snug as the home I had built for us in Nazareth, but still more comforting than a tent. The work had really just begun; I could see as much as a year or more employment here in Cairo on behalf of the Romans. Many of the workers were Egyptians and the head supervisors were all Romans, but Aram worked beside me often, and so I did not feel as completely alone. He was a carefree, joking sort of man, not at all formal or even religious, which was why he had left our homeland to see more of the world. And I have to credit the Romans for appreciating skilled work; the more Aram and I proved out our skills, the more they treated us if not with respect then at least without contempt. I even noticed a slight raise in payment as I was put in charge of some of the tasks before us. Though I was most comfortable with wood and had the most experience working it, I found my mason and metal working skills increased as I had more opportunities with those materials.

As the months passed by all that had come before in my life began to change or threaten to change. I was earning what seemed to me fair wages and I was trusted with skilled labor jobs only, unlike many others, who did the most difficult and dangerous jobs for little money or the slaves who had to work without any reward. I began to learn enough of the speech of both the Romans and the Egyptians to at least be able to communicate the basics back and forth, while Mary stayed mostly at home and only interacted with a few women while washing clothes or using the common cooking grounds. More and more I began to feel I was losing my Jewishness, which had been so much a natural part of whom I was that I had never before thought much about it. Now it became more and more difficult to follow the law: more difficult to keep kosher and impossible of course to get to the temple in Jerusalem or even to consult one of our priests or rabbis. Mary knew that some of these changes had to be accepted, she tried not to judge, but she could not accept my decision to work on the Sabbath.

"This was the first command the Lord gave to Moses. How can you not keep the day holy?" she questioned me. What choice did I have? We worked seven days a week; the Romans knew no day of rest, except for an occasional holiday to honor or celebrate one of their rascal gods, or a periodic half day off to keep the workers from collapsing from exhaustion. When I first tried to explain my need to have that one full day off per week I was laughed at. Aram had advised me not to push if I valued both my job and perhaps even my safety. The Romans did not insist ever that we honor their gods, but they drew a clear line when it came to interfering with their plans. I was too vital a worker to let have a day off each week and there were too many other workers who would have noticed and complained. My choice was clear. "You have been entrusted with the Messiah, the son of the Most High," Mary insisted "and the child isn't even a year old and this is how you instruct him in the ways of our people and our Lord?" she asked me with the closest tone she had to anger that I had to this point heard.

"If the Most High wished, he could strike Herod down today and deliver us back to our homeland. It is only his whim that leaves us here in a foreign land; it is his choice to make us raise his son, your son, in a place without a temple. My first responsibility, then, is to make sure his son does not starve to death. I'll do what I must to keep us all well-fed, safe and alive."

"Our Lord is merciful; surely, he will forgive you and not strike you down," Mary told me, her voice calm again, but her bright eyes remaining livid. "I'll pray for you, my husband, so that you might still be worthy of the trust our Lord has placed in you."

These were words I did not want to hear, particularly from a woman who had decided I must dedicate my life to being celibate, so that she might have no occasion for sin, a woman who caused me to be unclean as I would at times inevitably fall prey to the night dreams that would leave me in need of ritual cleansing. My wife's logic I still could not follow, and as more days passed, even as I should have been overjoyed by the boy's first steps, which happened while I was at work, in only the tenth month of his life, or weeks later his first word, which did thrill me when it happened, since the word was "Abba," father, I still found it easier, when I was away from Jesus and Mary, to feel more a part of the larger life I was leading as we built the new Babylon fortress.

Inside the walls of the old fortress was a teeming life of merchants and even entertainments. Sometimes I would go with Aram and the other workers to have some wine at a tavern that catered to the working men. This tavern was also frequented by women, again unlike anything that could happen back home. For both the Romans and Egyptians it seemed the zenut, the women who offered their bodies for sale, were accepted and even admired as more even than a necessary evil, and so they were allowed access to the men in certain places within the fortress. Aram would often joke with them, particularly he spoke with one named Rehema, a dark beauty who colored her face with vivid blue makeup and who dressed provocatively yet with style and pride. One late afternoon, not twenty minutes after we had completed the work for the day, a cause for celebration as another of the main walls of the fortress was now completely finished, Aram, I and some others who I had become friendly with, even though they were pagans, all sat around a table at the tavern, eating cheese and dates and drinking the blood red wine they favored in Cairo. Rehema came over to our table along with another woman, who she introduced as Safiya, and whose manner of dress indicated that she too was of Rehema's calling. Though dark she had somehow dyed her abundant hair almost to the color of straw and her eyes were even more dramatically highlighted by bright blue shadow. One of the Egyptians laughed upon hearing her name; he explained to Aram, who also laughed, before explaining to me, "In their language her name means 'one who is pure.'"

Aram soon after translated for me, since I could not keep up with Rehema's rapid speech, the next words she said to him: "My friend says she wants you to introduce her to your handsome companion. She wants to know why he has never visited with any of us; is he an unfriendly sort or is it that he prefers the company of men or perhaps camels?"

Aram laughed as he completed the translation, but before I could think to respond, he responded to her instead, and then told me what his response had been. "I told her you have a wife, a beautiful wife, and a healthy little boy, so you have no need for her affections, unlike myself who is alone in the world and would love to get to know this friend of hers."

Both women laughed at his response, but I could see that Safiya was looking at me intently and maybe trying to provoke me, little knowing how much easier it would be for that provocation than my friend Aram or anyone else could guess.

"Why do our women find you two Jews so attractive?" our friend Ammon joked with us.

"It must be because of our circumcisions," Aram laughed and the whole table exploded in laughter with him.

"Yes, that must be it," Safiya responded, unfazed, and she drew nearer to me and squeezed my right shoulder, giving me a look before she and her companion walked away from us. She left no physical mark, but I somehow feared Mary would be able to sense that contact when I came home that evening. Instead, she patiently accepted that I had come home late, that I was filled with wine, that I awoke the sleeping Jesus by my noisy entrance into our little home. We had really little to say to each other beyond how the work had proceeded or what new word Jesus had taken to saying. I felt as if our marriage was already falling apart and there were no angels or holy spirits to help us keep it in place As I took my place on the mat I slept in while Mary and the child slept in an adjoining bed, I thought of my beautiful, distant wife and how little her forbidden body could protect me from thoughts of the harlot Safiya.

Chapter Twelve

More months passed. I most often now worked as foreman on the various projects connected to completing the fortress; I had men under my essential command, the Romans being somewhat military in almost all things, and so I was able to have Aram as my assistant and interpreter a role he did not mind at all, of course, as it involved much less hard labor than he was accustomed to. My pay was more than fair; the attitude of the Romans themselves towards me, particularly as I learned more of their language and advanced their agenda, grew more and more towards respect. Still, all of this success did not make things any better between me and Mary. How could they? I worked long hours, spending all those hours with just one other Jewish person, and Aram was not a bit religious. Away from our customs and rituals, a part now of the world of the Romans, I was losing more and more my allegiance to what Mary was all about and though the little boy cared for me, I knew he was not my son, and I even sometimes questioned why he should be my responsibility. Mary became more and alarmed by how I talked, but there was no way to lessen the gulf between us. She remained as forbidden a fruit as Adam had ever experienced, except she was no Eve; she never attempted to tempt me into any wrong doing. I began to tell myself that I needed to be with another woman, any woman, if I were to continue to manage keeping my hands off of this "blessed ever Virgin" I had been tricked into marrying. Yet, how could adultery be preferable to convincing my wife she was mistaken and that we were meant to share a normal marriage and maybe even a comfortable life in Egypt? And so I tried again.

Unusually strong winds had made work difficult that day and so the Romans in their wisdom had given us a rare half day off. Instead of heading for the tavern with my friends, I decided to go directly home, preferring a chance to set Mary on a better path than to once again tempt myself with the women I would find at the tavern. Mary seemed surprised to see me and perhaps even a little annoyed. The child was asleep and she apparently had been deep in prayer. It was only then I remembered that it was once again the Jewish Sabbath, which would not end until the sun went down.

"Have you decided for once to honor the Sabbath, my husband? Even though only a few hours remain, it's never too late to go back to the ways of our people, to keep holy the Lord's day."

Though she might have meant these words with kindness and even hope, my own thoughts were far away from religious observation, so I took her speech as an attempt to blame me for my sins.

"Mary, I agree completely," I began. "It really is never too late to wrong a right. After all that's what our annual Day of Atonement is all about, right? So, really, I've come home early to see if you could maybe somehow, God willing and all that, come to your senses."

"In what way do you mean?"

"You know, by maybe being ready to recognize the duty you owe to your lawful husband."

"Please, not that again, Joseph, especially on the Sabbath," she pleaded, with what seemed like genuine pain in her voice. "I have told you, again and again, how sad it makes me for you to have to live this way."

"Does it really sadden you? It seems to me that it's only I who suffer. Have you no feelings for me at all, my Virgin wife? Or is desire impossible in one so perfect?"

"Joseph, please, don't."

"And speaking of the Sabbath, you a woman who knows the law so well, knows that it's a mitzvah to have relations with your spouse on the Sabbath. It's one of the few Sabbath activities the Most High has put his blessing upon. So I've come home just in time, haven't I?"

She stepped back away from me, almost without realizing it, as if she now feared this man she had chosen for her spouse, over the objections of her own parents. "Don't make a mockery of our holy day. Do you pray three times a day? Are you keeping our dietary laws? You can't pick and choose as it pleases you."

"And yet," I said, even as I stepped towards her, "even if I was the most law following Jew in the history of our people, there would still be no union with my spouse, Sabbath or no, isn't that right, virgin mother?"

"I have kept myself from all earthly desire and I wish you too could do the same. I am the handmaiden of the Most High; I must do only his will."

"Enough with the handmaiden," I shouted suddenly. "What of the wife?"

"Please, Joseph, your shouting will wake up Jesus."

"Let him awaken. Perhaps in his Messiah's wisdom he can explain to me the will of his father, his real father. Why did you or he need me at all? You could have stayed with your rich family and I never would have had to come to this strange land. Instead we are to continue deceiving everyone of the child's true nature, only I to know I've been cuckolded by the Holy Spirit."

"Please, Joseph, this is blasphemy. This comes from all your time with the Romans and ..."

"Be quiet, woman, while your husband speaks," I shouted at my wife, as I grabbed her by the wrists. "Are you going to end this madness? How can this be a proper household to raise any child, must less the Messiah? How am I to be any kind of father with no rights as a husband, no love or affection from my bride? How is it possible, my perfect wife?"

As I said these last words, I loosened, rather than tightened my grip on my spouse. One look into her beautiful, tearful grey-blue eyes took all my resilience away. My last words were said accompanied by my own tears, as I knelt down to her, knowing that there was no way we could lead a normal life, and no way I could blame her, she who had been visited by the Angel Gabriel, she who prophets had foretold would suffer much for this son of hers who slept oblivious to all that future suffering.

"I'm so sorry, my husband," Mary said, still looking at me with those sinless eyes. "I believe the Lord will make you strong; I'll need your help, so much help; the Lord must know what he is doing."

"Yes, yes, my wife, perhaps he does. I'm sorry to have disturbed your prayers. I have to go back to work now."

Yes, I lied and took the fifteen-minute walk over to the tavern, where I knew my friends would still be. All along my walk I thought to myself: Mary must remain without sin, must be perfect. Her son is the son of the Most High; how will he ever be capable of sin? But I, Joseph, a mere craftsman, who would ever demand moral perfection from me? In fact, if I was to remain with my two perfect housemates, the only way I could continue without wanting to kill myself would be to remain human and accept the sins that came with that humanity. If the Most High for some reason really wanted his son to have a human father, then I could just be myself. And since Mary was convinced that included never touching my wife, how could I be blamed if I sought some relief? Many of the Romans and Egyptians I had come to know saw nothing wrong in consorting with women who were not their wives. And even back in Nazareth there were certainly women like these, though their lives were less comfortable and the judgments against them more common. I had myself pretty convinced before I ever took my first drink of wine that early evening, that I would only be doing what my human nature expected of me, and where did I get that nature if not from the Most High?

For months Safiya had inflamed my dreams, though we had never spoken again after that one encounter. I still often saw her in the tavern, usually flirting with her aggressive and even outrageous style with one man or another. When I located Aram and the others and they found me a seat at their table, with pounding on my back and cheers for my change of heart in joining them, I soon after saw Safiya approaching us, almost as if she knew what had happened back home. She looked more beautiful than ever, having let her hair go back to its natural, almost black color, and having toned down her make-up until it almost looked like a fully natural enhancement of her face and eyes. She looked at me and then came over, putting one hand, whose fingernails were painted in a dark purple hue, on my shoulder, as she said: "So, it's the Galilean again. Have you decided the benefits of this place surpass those of your own home?"

"Off with you, tempter of man," Aram laughed, even as he roughly though playfully took her hand off my shoulder. "I've told you this one's taken. He comes here for fellowship with his workers, not to stray from his bride."

"Is this craftsman mute? Why is it I do not hear these words coming from his own mouth? And are you his assistant in all things, Aram, or are there things he can take into his own crafty hands?" she asked Aram with a smirk.

"Go, woman, I cannot compete with your viper's tongue," Aram laughed again. "If Joseph responds not a word to your overtures, let that silence be word enough."

"Yes, I'll take that advice," Safiya smiled. "I'll take that silence for all that it may be worth."

She withdrew from our table but not before letting a portion of her loose veil go over my face as she departed. Hours later I left the tavern, having stayed even after Aram advised we depart. He knew we needed our rest for the long work day ahead, but I told him I'd stay to finish my last goblet, which I did not want to rush. I remained in part because I was unsure I could walk a steady path back home in the darkness and in part because a part of me was hoping Safiya might return. Not seeing her anywhere inside, I decided finally to leave. I was not one minute into the journey towards home when I heard a voice behind me: "Craftsman, your walk staggers you like a man unsure. Won't you come and take some refreshment with me; I can give you something to steady yourself."

Still without saying a word back to her, I let her guide me like a man who has broken his leg and needs someone to support him, and soon we were in her house, itself a kind of temporary barracks constructed by the Romans, which she explained she shared with three other women, whom the Romans must have considered a necessary part of the work force. We found none of the other three at home.

"But what if they return?" I spoke my first words.

"In my own room we will have privacy, even should they return. Leave all your worries at the threshold, my poor, lonely craftsman."

In a moment more I was sitting on a bed, softer than any I had sat upon before, with ruby colored sheets and at the head of the bed large soft pillows with matching pillow-cases of deep red. I looked at Safiya who sat next to me, as if she were waiting for me to initiate what was to come. "I have never been with a woman before," I blurted out before I realized how strange that admission would sound coming from a married man with a child.

"Truer words you've never spoken, Galilean," Safiya laughed. "After you have spent one hour with me, you'll agree that I am your first real woman, nothing like that saintly child who keeps your son in breast milk."

"What do you know of Mary?"

"I know enough, craftsman. I know you're here."

"I don't know how much payment you expect," I hesitated further.

"You're making a mistake in talking of money now. Such talk will undo our passion. And it's a passion I feel for you Joseph, one I have felt since the first time I saw you, and your big, dark eyes, reflecting so much sadness and loneliness."

"All that you could tell from my eyes? Are you some kind of sorceress?"

"No, but it doesn't take magic to know what a man is feeling. And after we're done you will not know how to repay me, but you will, again and again. But first, I want to be sure your own passion has carried you to my bed, not too much wine or anger with your woman. I want you to commit to me this moment," Safiya demanded as she grabbed me by the hand and looked deeply into those very eyes of mine.

"What do you mean, commit?" I asked and instinctively moved myself away from such commitment and from range of Safiya's touch.

She didn't try to get closer but continued to explain: "From the Roman courtesans, I've learned much of what a man really wants. These women tell me in Rome they are honored like generals, like statesmen. They recite poetry, they talk philosophy; they are not just objects of lust. And so too I've come to want more. And it's you I know who can supply it – one look in your tragic eyes reveals it."

Safiya then reasserted herself, as she first put her lips to my cheek and caressed my beard with her hand. I looked her over, saw her breasts awaiting my touch, looked down to where her waist was exposed, looked even to her feet where her sandals let show that her toenails were painted the same shade of purple as her long fingernails. "Do you know any poetry, Galilean?" she asked next.

I was caught in a kind of frightening ecstasy as I placed my arms around her bare waist. Still, she seemed to be waiting for something more, was actually serious about the poetry and so I found myself quoting words from Solomon himself, our sacred words, in our sacred language to this beautiful pagan.

"How beautiful are your sandaled feet, princess! The curves of your thighs are like jewelry, the handiwork of a master. Your navel is a rounded bowl, it never lacks mixed wine. Your waist is a mound of wheat surrounded by lilies. Your breasts are like two fawns, twins of a gazelle."

Safiya smiled her approval, and kissed me once on the mouth, before having more to say: "Ah, the 'Song of Solomon,'" she correctly noted, and she said the title not in Egyptian but in the language of my own people. "It's my favorite of all. Don't look so surprised, craftsman; I have been with many, many men, in many places – giving them what they most need. I speak four languages well and know a smattering of many more. Here, listen, if you don't believe me, I even know the response to your seducing words: 'Your mouth is like fine wine flowing smoothly for my love, gliding past my lips and teeth. I belong to my love and his desire for me.'"

With her quoting of the sacred words my amazement was complete. Now our union, my first with any woman, seemed inevitable; Safiya sat on my lap and began to softly nibble my ear. The sensations I felt as I groped my hands on her back, were more wonderful than even I'd imagined they would be, and I felt as if I might ignite any moment into flames. I kissed her cheeks and then her mouth; she seemed in no hurry, but kept her eyes focused on my own. She then repeated, in the sacred language: "I belong to my love and his desire for me."

That I should be in the bedroom of this beautiful woman with the opportunity finally to experience what had been stolen from me in my rights as a lawful husband was amazing to me. What happened next, though, was even more amazing. As I looked back in Safiya's eyes I didn't see a woman of her spoken experience and worldliness. I saw how young she was, perhaps even younger than Mary, and I thought of all she had been through to have suffered so many men. Hearing her again say the words from our sacred language, the beautiful words of one of our Kings, made me suddenly ashamed. That I had used those words, words I had in fact memorized to one day share with my spouse on my wedding night, that I had used them to secure sex was bad enough, but that she said them back to me not with cynical ease but as if she really did love me, this made me think of other words from our holy books: "You must not defile your daughter by making her a prostitute, or the land will be prostituted and filled with depravity." Even as I continued to feel passion, even as Safiya continued to touch me and stir me, I knew I'd be left only with shame and regret if I continued. It was as if a guardian angel were at my side, showing me that the aftermath of this passion would only be shame and regret and that it was not too late to escape this adultery. I saw this beautiful woman and did not want her at this cost, a price higher than any amount of money she could have demanded. With a resolve that had to come from the Most High, I lifted this lovely woman off my lap, placed her back on her bed and made ready to leave. I thanked the Lord I was so full of wine, that my senses were dulled enough to make resisting Safiya possible. Otherwise overwhelmed and overstimulated with poetry, plus Safiya's perfume and incredible face and form, I might never have managed to try to escape:

"This is a mistake. I cannot be with you. I have a wife I must be faithful to."

"You knew that when you came here, Joseph," she responded, though she made no move to drag me back onto her bed. "What has changed your mind? Surely, I am pleasing to you."

"You are a beautiful woman, Safiya, you deserve more than I am able to give."

"Don't deny yourself this pleasure, foolish man," she encouraged. "Don't deny me this moment either, for I can tell you are no ordinary man."

"If that's really true, I should not do the expected, the ordinary thing, I have to rise above this unholy passion. I cannot degrade what should be holy by giving in to my earthly needs."

Safiya's eyes lit up with fury, but her voice remained controlled as she stood up and looked me squarely in the eyes. "I'm never one to beg or to give second chances. No amount of money offered will get you back in my bed if you abandon it now," Safiya added, but with less anger and more sadness that I would have guessed possible. I felt all the more pain knowing that my refusal was actually causing her pain. But I could not dwell on that:

"Thanks be to the Lord, then, since I don't know if I could otherwise escape you. Your beauty really is not to be measured. I'll pray that you might be delivered from this life to something more fitting to that beauty."

"Foolish man. There is no higher calling than to deliver man from his sorrow. Don't stay married to yours. There's still a chance; you have not yet crossed the threshold again."

But I remained foolish and I walked out into the night. I remained mostly innocent of the carnal touch of a woman, but my having overcome the temptation seemed the most empty of all victories.

Chapter Thirteen

From that evening forward, I avoided the tavern entirely. I spent time with my wife and the child and tried to be the best father I could. Mary was pleased though she still was saddened that I continued to work on our Sabbath. Though I had avoided the crisis of being unfaithful to my marriage vows, I still enjoyed too much the respect and payment I received for my work to consider abandoning both by keeping the Lord's day holy. Still, I enjoyed my time with Mary and Jesus, who grew strong and spoke at eighteen months better than many three-year-olds could. While I was gone at work, Mary spoke to him much of sacred things; his Hebrew was even more advanced than his Aramaic thanks to his mother's devotions. I'll confess, though, that I received more joy when he learned the words for hammer and craftsman and when we would find a little time to walk over to the Nile and try our luck at fishing. The first little fish he caught, two months before his second birthday, a tilapia that wasn't more than six inches, pleased me and I think him more than any Bible story. "Is this a keeper, Papa?" he sang out with joy as he got it to shore. Whatever his real father wanted from his son, this future Messiah, this king of kings, I could only give him the things I knew best and they seemed to please him well.

Aram remained a good friend in spite of my absence from the tavern. The truth was he seemed relieved that I as a married man would now discontinue the possibility of giving in to its temptations. Though he had chosen this wandering, non-religious life for himself, he didn't want me to join him in it; I had a wife and son, after all. Mary sensed his good influence and happily suggested I invite him sometimes to share a meal with us.

It was the second such visit, just after we had finished a nice meal when the four of us sat together around the sturdy little supper table I had fashioned myself when Aram surprised me by asking Jesus which of the stories from our holy books he liked best so far.

"My favorite is Jonah," the boy replied.

"Ah, that's just because he likes anything to do with fishing," I chuckled.

"But in Jonah it's the great fish that catches the man, not the other way around," Mary pointed out, also with a smile.

"Yes, well, it's one of my favorites too," Aram nodded in agreement.

"And why is that, my friend?" I asked.

"Well, it has adventure, it has a sea monster, but mostly it has the best lesson of any of our many stories."

"I'm so happy to know of your knowledge of our scriptures," Mary smiled. "Someday I know we will return to our homeland and the ways of our people; do you long for that day too, Aram?"

"It's because of Jonah that I don't worry so much," Aram replied with an actual wink.

"Explain yourself," I encouraged him.

"Perhaps I should take Jesus to wash up now and get ready for bed," Mary suggested.

"No, I mean no harm," Aram laughed. "It's just that poor Jonah tries so hard to escape the will of the Most High, but there is no place he can go to escape him. And Jonah is taught his lesson and does the Lord's will; he goes to Nineveh. And so I'm thinking, when the Lord wants me to return to his ways, when he is tired of my travels and my lifestyle, he'll surely let me know."

"Aram, our Lord watches over us always and has kept you a righteous man even in your wanderings. But let's hope you won't need to be swallowed by a whale before you'll come back to our faith," Mary chided him.

"Could someone really be swallowed by a whale?" Jesus asked, with a kind of hope in his voice.

"All things are possible with the Most High," Aram assured him.

"Amen," Mary said, and I knew Aram would always be welcome in our home.

"You're a really lucky man, Joseph," Aram told me, as I walked him part of the way back to his own dwelling. "To have such a beautiful wife, such a smart and happy little boy, such blessings, and each week, it seems more respect and reward from the Romans. You really are blessed."

As I lie down on my mat, alone as always, as I tried to sleep that night, I wondered what Aram would think if he knew about Mary's ever Virgin status, much less how it would strike him to find out who Jesus's real father was. Still, I recognized that in many ways I was lucky, though it was hard to reconcile the family joys with my success with the Romans, since Mary still longed more for my return to Sabbath observances than any amount of money or prestige my work would garner me. And about a month later all of that came to an unexpected climax.

The work on the new fortress was pretty much completed. Mary seemed to be hoping this would mean I could end my connection to the Romans of many gods and return a complete and true observer of our own faith. Weekly, she would remind me of my responsibilities to our son; she took to calling him our son and it seemed petty ever to correct her, particularly since he himself did not know he wasn't actually of my own blood. I loved him more each day, and we had certainly been able to save some money, so that a time of unemployment was no longer as worrisome as it had been when we arrived in Cairo. Even then Mary had balked about the move, since it had taken us so much further from our homeland, but the move to Cairo had saved us from starvation and educated me in the way of the Romans. And so it was that I came home one day with big news for Mary, but news I knew I would have to sell like the most skilled street peddler.

I waited one evening until the child was asleep to begin: "It's official now, my bride, the work of the great fortress is completed."

"I can tell by the expression on your face, my husband, that you have other news for me then that," Mary said.

"Yes, and big news at that. The Romans are doing a great deal of construction in the city of Palmyra, which has grown great as a crossroads of trade, and they want me to travel next with them to that great place and be in charge of a construction crew. We leave in a few days' time."

"We leave? Does that we include your wife and son?"

"Of course it does, and I'm told accommodations will be more lavish for us there. The Romans know how to treat their skilled laborers."

"You forget, my husband, that the Romans keep our people in subjugation and that your son has been born to be a Messiah of your people, to deliver us from the power of their rule. They are pagans and should not have such sway with you."

"They are in charge and they have respect for me and my work," I answered, defensively, "and I need to work to keep us alive. Plus, though I say they have asked me to work for them, when the Romans ask, they don't expect you to say no. Since we cannot go home, what difference is it what strange country we inhabit? I'm told, in fact, that Palmyra is much closer to Jerusalem than Cairo is, and closer still to Nazareth. Plus the people there speak a dialect of Aramaic. I don't know why you would object."

"To journey back towards Jerusalem is good," Mary nodded, "but the journey towards the Temple has to be of the spirit or else the physical distance doesn't matter."

"We're going," I declared. "In two days or so. It's as simple as that."

"Nothing is as simple as that," Mary said, with almost a mysterious tone. "But I will not fight you, my husband, but only pray."

Did Mary know what was coming? It wouldn't surprise me. After all she and the Holy Spirit had quite a history. And so it was that as I slept I was once more visited by the angel Shlomo.

"Big news, craftsman," he started, and this time what was strange was that I knew I was dreaming but also that he really was there in my dream and that whatever he told me had to be true.

"Yes, I know – we're headed for the great city of Palmyra."

"That's almost true," he chuckled, but then he rolled his eyes in a most unangelic fashion.

"What do you mean, almost?" I had to ask.

"It's a long way back to Judah, so it's nice you'll have a Roman escort much of the time. But you're veering off with Mary and Jesus and headed back home."

"And why would I do that?" I still stayed stubborn.

"Because that monster King Herod is dead. Because Jesus needs to be back among his people. Because the will of the Most High must be served. Are those enough reasons, craftsman?" Shlomo asked and then pushed my forehead with his right, angelic hand, just strong enough to remind me whose emissary I was conversing with.

"I guess they'll have to do," I sighed, knowing, like Jonah before me, there was no denying the will of our Lord. "This will make Mary very happy."

"There's that," Shlomo nodded, "plus it will get you away from all these pagans – you've really been pushing it, what with the Romans and the harlots and all. Our God is a merciful God. But it's time to get a grip, man. Time to be the father you were meant to be."

I woke up resolved to give it a try.

Chapter Fourteen

It wasn't easy getting away from that Roman caravan. Somehow we managed to slip off in the cool and scary darkness of night. I worried about one cry from Jesus, one bray from Sarah giving us away, but both remained silent as we put some distance between us and what would have been a prosperous future in Palmyra and beyond. Instead, we were once more vagabonds, on our own, with limited supplies, headed back towards the Holy Land.

When we reached the home of Ruth and Micah they were as kind as ever in greeting us, and so happy to see Jesus that I thought Ruth would never stop crying.

"These are the people who took us in when you were born, my son," Mary told the child and he looked at our friends and said: a simple "Thank you," that in its calm maturity still seemed like something beyond a two-year old's range. Perhaps it was because of the deep thanks that registered in his eyes, which had the same amazing blue-grey color as his mother's. And somehow I was more pleased than chagrined when both our friends said that, except for the eyes, the child mostly took after me. After all, the Most High could make him look like anyone he wanted to, so why not me?

"But you can't stay here long," Micah advised me, even as he was helping me to get Sarah fed and watered after our long journey.

"Why is that? I was going to get ready to try to convince Mary again about why Bethlehem, being so close to the holy city, made more sense for us than Nazareth. Have you no work for me?" I asked.

"It's not that," Micah assured me, but I still pressed the point.

"I imagine you've gotten along fine without me these two years, but I've learned a lot from working with the Romans and some of it might be useful to you."

"I'm telling you it's not that. I'd love you to stay and so would Ruth; it's because I care so much for you that I tell you to leave. Herod's son Archelaus, the new king of Judah is worse than his father. He taxes us so heavily that all the profit I might have made from the inn I constructed in Jerusalem goes to enrich him only. His cruelty and tyranny are beyond belief. He has had men beaten, some even killed, for almost no reason at all."

"But why would I ever have any trouble with him? He'd never even know we were here; kings don't visit Bethlehem, right?" I reasoned.

"I tell you no one is safe from his whims, not even children, especially not little children. He seems certain somehow that his father's massacre of all those innocent infants and toddlers didn't murder his rival. If he somehow found out Jesus was born here right around the time those strange Magi visited the result would be another murder. I tell you, go back to Nazareth, where Mary has family and Archelaus's brother, Herod Antipas, is too comfortable and lazy to bother about anyone else but himself. There you will be safe from this monster."

When I told Mary that night what Micah had said, she did not seem a bit surprised.

"All along it has been destined that Jesus should be a Galilean, should be from Nazareth. I never doubted the will of the Most High. You must conform yourself to his will, my husband, and all will be well."

Mary always kept her tone just a hair away from smug. I could never find fault with her attitude towards me, which somehow made it all the more maddening. After another sad goodbye to our friends, and a brief stop in Jerusalem, we were once more on the road, though this time plentifully supplied by our generous friends. Several days later, we found ourselves at my in-laws door.

Both Joachim and Anne had aged far more than the two years we'd been gone should have warranted. Joachim's hair had silvered twice as much as when we'd last seen him and Anne looked more frail and at first even a bit lost, as she tried to comprehend that her prayers had actually been answered, that the little boy with the amazing blue-grey eyes was actually her grandson. The loud praising of the Lord and cries of joy lasted as long as one might expect, but it wasn't much more than a moment after we had sat down that Joachim started up on me.

"I'll never understand why you had to flee to Egypt. Why so far away? I think you would have been safer and much happier too, just to come back to us here."

Joachim really didn't expect an explanation or argument; he was just going to lament his son-in-law's failings, finally now with that actual son-in-law in sight. What could I tell him anyway? An angel made me do it? His grandson was the future Messiah and the son of the Most High and so we took our orders from a higher source? Of course, he didn't blame Mary a bit for our absence, but I never expected him too. So I decided just to take whatever he needed to vent upon me, which was convenient because I had a lot more coming my way.

"That worthless apprentice of yours ran your little shop into the ground in a matter of a few months, with his shoddy craftsmanship and his lazy attitude."

"But I asked Jude to keep an eye on him and on my place," I countered. "I can't believe he would let him get away with anything."

"Well, as to that, I'm sorry to have to be the one to tell you, but your good friend the tailor was waylaid by robbers on his way back from his birth town, where he too had to travel because of the Roman census. He's been dead since even before you left Bethlehem for Egypt."

My shock and sadness over this sudden news about the death of my only real friend in Nazareth I had to keep to myself for the moment, since Joachim wasn't finished complaining.

"So I had to close your place up before that worthless idiot could run away with all your tools. Your house I've been renting to a family, since it seemed a waste to have it just sitting there, a good, sturdy little house, I'll give you that, and I had no idea whether you would ever bring my daughter back to me, and you know I can't just throw those renters out now that you're back, but, luckily, there's plenty of room here, so you can…"

It was Mary who interrupted her father's tirade. "No, father, that is very generous of you, but we won't intrude on your hospitality. We'll stay only until Joseph can build us a new little hut and get his shop back up and going. His skills have only increased from his time away; I'm sure we'll be fine."

Any other daughter would not have had a chance against a team like Joachim and Anne, but Mary's presence had only grown stronger since she had become a mother, so, as usual, they did not choose to argue with her. I don't know exactly why she chose not to live with her parents in their lavish home, but I was pretty happy with the decision though I tried not to make that too obvious to my in laws.

We ended up staying at Joachim and Anne's place for two months before the little home I put together (and to be fair, Joachim gave me access to the finest materials and at times a few of his workers) was deemed fit for their daughter and grandson. Jesus they doted on almost mercilessly, but, like his mother, he had patience and took every attempt to smother him with concern and worry as the act of love that I guess it really was. As I expected, nothing I thought fit for the boy, whether it was visiting my workshop and job site with me (the walk was too long; the construction mess no place for a little boy) or just not loading up on dates or figs before dinner ("Let the boy eat") was ever okay with his grandparents. Knowing we would soon be free of their daily interference was the only thing that kept me sane, though I knew that even after we left their house, we'd be seeing plenty of them at our own home and be expected to make theirs our own second living space.

My business wasn't booming, but the town needed a skilled craftsman and my reputation had already been established before I left and the people of Nazareth had been suffering from the poor work of others during my absence. I took pleasure in my work, since there was little to take at my in-laws home, aside from the rich food and wine. And since I could receive no physical love from my spouse, I put all my energy and drive into making anything I fashioned the best it could possibly be. It wasn't long before the people of Nazareth were singing the praises of Joseph the Craftsman, and they were by and large a difficult people who didn't do a lot of singing.

It didn't take much time for me to get back to the routines of life as an observant Jew, so much so that my days with the Romans seemed as if they had been a dream. We followed the kosher laws, we kept holy the Sabbath, we prayed three times daily, we taught the little boy more and more of the words of our prophets and elders; his ability to soak up Hebrew and even seem to know what he was saying when he repeated the various prayers and blessings made his grandparents especially proud. Mary and I took it more as a matter of course, since his real father had to have a hand in it. Still, in most ways he remained a very normal little boy; he didn't work miracles or speak like an adult and when he ran and fell, he skinned his knees and those knees bled real blood. Still, he was a good boy, a very good boy, and I wondered at how happy and yet obedient he always was.

"Why should you be surprised?" Mary asked me one evening after we had put him to bed. "He's the son of the Most High. He will be incapable of sin, even as I must always strive to be."

"When you say that, do you mean his father will prevent him ever from having occasion to sin? Will he only then appear to be a person, when really he will never be tempted to do wrong?" I wasn't trying to cause an argument. I really wanted to know and had already given a lot of thought to what Jesus would be like.

"I am of course wholly human and yet I have dedicated myself to a life without sin to try to be worthy of what the Lord has asked of us. This too should be your goal, my husband, as difficult as it will always be. Our son, though, since he is of the Most High, I don't understand how he could ever be tempted to do something the Lord condemns, either large or small. How could the son of God ever sin?"

"But you don't know that for certain, right? No angel has forecast his behavior for you?" I asked.

"No, I don't know for certain," Mary responded, with as close to an eye roll as a sinless person could manage, "but how can the son of the Most High ever be guilty of sin? It doesn't make any sense."

"Well, maybe the rules for common men do not apply to the son of the Most High," I suggested. "Maybe he can do whatever he wants, but since he's the Lord's son, for him it won't be a sin?"

"No, Joseph, that cannot be," Mary said, though she sounded a bit less certain, as she sat herself on a chair I had fashioned myself.

"Why not?" I wondered.

"My son must be pure and holy and good. I'm sure the Lord will help him never to do a cruel or selfish thing."

"If he's a person and so far he seems much to me like a little person, he's going to have to deal with the Devil just like the rest of us," I said, and I put my hand in Mary's as I said it, to show her I was only like her, a parent trying to figure out what the future held for our son. And, yes, I thought completely now in terms of "our" son, since I was the only father he knew. "Now he is always so ready to do whatever we ask of him. I've not once even thought of disciplining him – there has been no need. But won't he sometimes disobey or do something foolish, as all children do? Won't I have to fulfill my role as father?"

Mary stood up from the chair and let go of my hand as if it were on fire. "Your role as his father is to love him and teach him the ways of our people. Are you telling me you'd even think of striking little Jesus?" she asked, eyes flashing.

"No, I'm asking you how else you expect me to fulfill the role of father that the angels have ordained for me, if I don't fully act the part of a father. Isn't obedience and discipline part of that role?"

"It's crazy, Joseph, to think a person can strike the son of the Most High. You must never lay a hand on him in anger. I'm sure he'll never give you cause to be angry; he is the anointed one; he won't be like other boys."

"So why does he need an earthly father at all? Or even an earthly mother. Why didn't our Lord just send him down fully grown, in no need of guidance or protection? Or why didn't he just come himself?"

Mary seemed to calm down a little, saw me less as someone threatening her offspring and more a man confused, and wanting to do what was right.

"I don't have all the answers; you've been visited by an angel more recently than I have. I just know all that has been done and is to come is to fulfill the prophecies and to serve the ways of our Lord. I just know it can't be right to think our son will ever be subject to sin, will ever not honor his father and mother."

I could see Mary was set in her view. I still wasn't sure. Since the Lord had decreed I should just be a sham husband, I guess it was consistent that I should also not have the usual fatherly role. Still, this boy, this Jesus, loved it when I took him fishing, wanted to learn all about my craft, its tools and skills and process, asked me questions about animals and birds and why the rain and wind came only now and then. He was the son of the Most High, I remained convinced, but his real father was at least at present supplying him with no answers. It was all being left to me. And so I thought I would take it day by day, and give him all the love I could, but if at times he needed discipline, for his own good, I was ready to supply it, no matter what Mary thought, until some angel or the Lord himself might come to stop my mistake. I prayed I'd not make too many in trying to be some kind of father to little Jesus, the anointed one, the Messiah, the little boy who called me father.

Chapter Fifteen

More than six years passed with amazingly little change in our lives or circumstances. Though Anne, like Elizabeth, had had but one child and late in life, she
and Joachim seemed rejuvenated in their role as grandparents and were in good
health and full meddling mode the entire time. Jesus loved his grandparents, who
doted on him and bragged about him and predicted great things for him, though
Joachim probably saw him as a future heir to his large land and business holdings
rather than the savior of his people. Jesus continued to grow and showed real in-
telligence and a love of the holy scriptures, but I still got the impression that Joachim would prefer a future with Jesus the richest man in Nazareth, rather than
Jesus the rabbi or scholar. Mary and I never actually had a conversation about not
telling her parents anything of Jesus's destiny, much less his heritage, but somehow
it was a silent pact between us. I could only imagine how much less Joachim would
respect me if he knew who Jesus's real father was. Still, it was for our son's sake
more than my own, I felt, that we kept it to ourselves, which included saying nothing yet to Jesus about who he really was. And these unspoken understandings between me and Mary were part of what made us feel more and more like a couple.
I saw Mary was trying her best always to be both a good mother and a good wife
and her goodness was so genuine that it helped move me away, at least much of
the time, from continuing my resentment over her choice for us both to remain
perpetually celibate.

One day, a little more than a year after our return to Nazareth Mary had entered my workshop and asked me to come into the house for a talk. She had just
gotten the child to take a nap, which was becoming a rare event for our active and
always inquisitive son. She handed me a drink of water and we sat down together
in the little room I had furnished myself with a few of the most comfortable chairs
my skills could fashion. I wondered what could be troubling my wife, but I didn't
have long to wonder.

"Joseph, you wouldn't keep anything from me, would you?" she asked, with a
calm voice but a definite look of concern in her blue-grey eyes.

"What do you mean?" I asked, in a voice and tone that must have conveyed my genuine puzzlement. "You know I've remained faithful to you; you know I love our child, you know the business goes well enough, so what can be troubling you?"

"I know your heart well, my husband. My prayers have been answered since we left the temptations and hardship of Egypt. No woman could ask for a more loving, considerate husband, especially considering all I've asked you to accept."

"And I feel fully blessed to have been given the gift of responsibility for you and for our son. So what can you possibly think that I'm keeping from you?"

"Has there been no angel?" Mary blurted out. "I was so sure we would get further guidance, something to let us know if we're doing what we should be doing. I pray and pray for guidance but the Lord sends me no sign. You have been the one he has blessed with an angel many times. Surely, you would let me know what you have been told to do."

"Surely is right, Mary. Why would I keep such a secret? What would be my reason?" I asked.

"To protect me," Mary responded. "If your angel has told you something of the trouble ahead, has warned you of the trials to come or has spoken perhaps of my unworthiness, these things you might keep from me, out of love. But, please, spare me nothing, so that I can try to do better, so I too can know what is to come however sad."

Mary began to cry and her tears moved me so much that I could for a moment not articulate the words I longed to say to assure and soothe her. Of course I soon had her convinced that I too was angel-less and without a clue as to what might be in any of our futures. Further I assured her that a better mother and spouse had never before walked the earth. This reassurance she received with grace and complete belief. She knew now that I would never lie to her or hold anything back. This conversation served as a further growing of our trust and love for each other. From that point forward one of us might occasionally ask the other, almost playfully, at the start of a new day "Any angels?" and receive the response, "Not yet, my love." Of course, I was becoming more convinced each day the only angel I needed for guidance and support was Mary herself.

We raised our son as any loving, religious parents would have done, and Jesus continued to be both obedient and happy. One time I did come to use my hands on him, when he was four and twice got too close to a fire I was using to do some metal work. The second time I hit him, not very hard, and just on his right hand, as I said, "No, my son, you must not get so close to the fire." I startled him with my actions and he looked at me with tears in his eyes and genuine contrition in his voice as he said, "I'm sorry, Papa, to displease you. The fire is so beautiful but I knew not to touch it. I'm very sorry."

Though no angry voice from Heaven or punishing lightning bolt attacked me for having struck the son of the Most High that was the last time I hit the child. His tears were all for having gone against my wishes, for having disappointed me. His eyes were full of love and respect and worry that I had been hurt by his actions or was now disappointed in him. I assured him: "There isn't anything to cry about, son. I was just trying to protect you from getting burnt. A bad burn hurts a lot more than a little slap on the hand. I'm not angry." Who could be angry with such a son? He seemed always to understand how difficult my life was, though he could know nothing of my relationship with his mother and I didn't complain about his grandparents in front of him. He seemed to sense I needed a friend and he was going to make sure, young as he was, that he would be that faithful companion.

Three times a year a faithful Jew must travel to the temple in Jerusalem if at all possible and our circumstances and Mary's insistence both made those trips a given for us. The first few years we left the child with his grandparents, who had the excuse of age not to travel so far and the happy consequence of time alone with their grandson. From the time of his fifth birthday onward , though, we took him with us in part so he could get to know his Aunt Elizabeth and cousin John (Zechariah had passed away when our child was only three). And so it was that Jesus, now a little more than eight years old, was again accompanying us first to Ain Karim, and then with Elizabeth and her son, to the temple in Jerusalem.

Jesus was always excited to go on these trips. He loved the temple in all its grandness, but he even seemed to love the daily travel, since his ever richer grandfather made sure we always had the best of supplies and in addition to our still trusty Sarah, a camel to convey us and those supplies. Jesus seemed to have a special connection to animals. Camels can be dangerous or in the very least disagreeable, but this one let Jesus pet him and talk soothingly to him without the slightest sign

of disapproval. For all of his life so far, Jesus got along well with all of God's creatures, with only one real exception, and that was his crazy cousin John.

And so when we arrived at Ain Karim I could tell Jesus was nervous. Mary very
much wanted the two cousins to be close and Jesus understood that and tried his
best, but to me he had confided that his slightly older and considerably larger
cousin frightened him sometimes.

"Does he bully you? Does he hit you or say mean things?" I had questioned,
but Jesus responded,

"No, no nothing like that, father, but still somehow he scares me; he seems
happy to see me, but he says the strangest things and wants me to do odd things
with him."

"Like what?" I had insisted on knowing.

"Well, last year we went for a walk and we found a wild bee hive and he wanted
me to help him gather honey from it. When I was afraid he told me not to be a
baby, that the stings were worth it, but I didn't want to help, so he went after the
honey himself. He got stung more than a few times but he just laughed it off and
came back to me, his fingers dripping with honey and his hands filled with the
cone. He still laughed at me, called me a baby, but still he wanted to share the
honey with me and looked hurt when I wouldn't, so I did, I tried it, and that made
him somehow really happy."

"With wild honey you never can be sure what flowers it came from – you have
to be careful. Some of those flowers have things that can harm you. Maybe it's
wild honey that makes him act so crazy," I said, trying to joke Jesus into not being
worried.

"I think it's more than that," Jesus responded. "He makes me afraid, but still I
know he means me no harm. There's a wildness in his eyes, though, father, especially when he looks right at me, that makes me afraid. He seems to look right
through me or he looks at me and sees something more than can be there. And so
I don't think he ever wants to hurt me, but he still scares me sometimes."

I didn't share this information with my wife, who wanted the two boys to be
like brothers, which was also her cousin Elizabeth's attitude completely. Still, when
we got to their home and John wanted immediately to have Jesus run off with him
to play outside, I insisted Jesus needed first to rest and then Elizabeth offered us

food, so I kept them in my sight for as long as I could. I thought twice before having a slice of Cousin Elizabeth's famous "honey cake," but decided to believe she didn't get her honey from the same places as her son.

Cousin John looked more like a pagan savage than someone who could be the cousin of the son of the Most High. From spending almost all available hours outdoors he was as dark as an Egyptian, with once dark brown hair that had been reddened by the sun, hair he never seemed once to have had cut and that he kept tied up with twine in a long pony tail. His mother could not keep a cloak on him once he went outdoors and he would have preferred to remain that way inside as well. Though he was only months older than Jesus, he was inches taller, broader and very athletic; he outran Jesus easily after challenging him to foot races and giving Jesus the head start, and Jesus was a bit above average himself in foot speed and strong too from having spent hours with me in my workshop. He was no match for John, though, and that delighted his cousin, though there really was no sign he was bullying Jesus, at least not with threats or ugly words.

I had brought along our fishing poles, strong poles of my own construction, which we had used, with some success, during our trip to Ain Karim along the Jordan river. Since John had admired our poles when he saw them the year before, I had brought one along for him as well, along with a number of hooks and weights I had fashioned. He loved the pole, and he showed that love by giving me a bear hug with almost an adult's strength, but then he started jumping up and down and insisting he get to use his pole right away.

"But there is no water right nearby to fish in," his mother gently reminded him.

"Well, the river isn't very far, but, even better, we could get to the great sea in a day with our cousins' camel and donkey to help us," he exclaimed. "We could camp there and fish – imagine the great fish we might catch from the great sea itself. Please, we don't need to be in Jerusalem for a week! Please, mother, please Cousin Joseph, say you will, please!"

Jesus and I were avid fishermen, and the idea of a sea visit had certainly crossed my mind each time we visited Elizabeth: a real sea, an ocean really, and not the big lake we called a "sea" which we had fished a few times already back in Galilee. Still, I had never brought it up to Mary or Elizabeth, since I'd imagined they would not go for it. But now that John was begging and I could see Jesus's excitement at the idea, I looked at my wife, to try to gauge from her expression where she might stand on the topic. Seeing my gaze, she responded to it: "I think it's a great idea, if you don't stay away too long. Elizabeth and I can catch up while you three men go off and have an adventure together catching fish. What do you think, Elizabeth?"

Like her parents, Mary's cousin Elizabeth never argued with her, plus she obviously let her son do as he pleased, so her yes was almost an afterthought. Though I hadn't actually said a word about wanting to take the trip, soon it was settled, and we spent the rest of the evening preparing for the morning's upcoming travels.

If anyone thinks it might be fun to travel with two eight-year-olds, while trying to manage a donkey and a camel, I would invite them to try it for themselves. Jesus as always was trying to be helpful and do whatever I asked of him, but John was hard to control; "Can I guide the camel now cousin Joseph?" "Why can't I have more figs? I'm still hungry, mother always lets me have as many as I want – she says that's why I've grown so strong" "Why can't we travel at night? We're almost there aren't we? I don't want to wait until tomorrow." "Do camels really spit at people? What can we do to make him spit, Cousin Joseph? I bet I can dodge it – I'm fast, you know. Want to see?" He never stopped asking questions, fidgeting, coming close more than once to toppling our supplies, spooking our camel, falling into our camp fire. There wasn't a bit of bully to him, I realized; he was just a crazy kid, crazy with energy and spirit and life.

We found our way to the great sea road and soon after chose a spot to try our luck at fishing. I told the boys we could only fish for maybe four or five hours, as we had to get back to be in time for our temple visit in Jerusalem, and it had of course taken longer to get to the sea than John had guessed it would, so it was sure to take longer to get back as well. Both boys were disappointed; Jesus loved to fish and John didn't want his adventure to end so soon, but they knew I would not relent. I took out the poles, attached a bit of moldy cheese we had brought with us for bait, and we cast our lines into the water, at a spot where some rocks jutted into the sea, allowing us to cast into waters a bit deeper than we could reach from the sandy shore.

John hadn't fished before, plus he was so impatient always to be doing something, so every five minutes he shouted, "I have a bite," or "This time I'm sure Cousin Joseph," but of course he had just snagged some seaweed or, worse, gotten caught on some rocks. I spent more time trying to untangle or free his line than I could fishing. I'd hoped the cheese would attract at least some sort of bottom dwelling fish, but we had no luck with it, and this made John still more impatient. He left off fishing and started scouring the shore instead, looking for some living bait. After ten minutes or so of that, I had to leave off fishing, tell Jesus to follow, and run after him before he went too far away to be found. When we caught up, he was jumping with excitement. "Look at these little creatures. What are they? Can we use them for bait? Can we?"

"Those are called crabs, I believe. They're unclean. You'd better leave them alone, John," I told him.

"Unclean to eat, but not to touch, father," Jesus informed me.

"How does he know things like that?" John wondered.

"He's becoming very learned," I responded, both with pride and some embarrassment. "But that's right, you can touch them, but not eat them. Some types are bigger and the pagans eat them."

"Well, most of these fish in this sea must be pagans," John decided, with a wild laugh. "So they'll want to eat these little guys, right? It'll serve them right for not keeping kosher, if we catch them. And if we catch those fish, we're allowed to eat them, right?"

"So long as they have fins and scales," Jesus reminded us. "And so long as we are sure to totally remove the bait from any proper fish we might catch."

"So, that means we can use these crab things for bait, right? Better than that smelly cheese for sure," John concluded.

And so we collected a number of small crabs, with light blue-green shells; I warned the boys about not getting pinched. Jesus avoided any harm, but John got caught a few times, and it made him yelp, but then he laughed it off, almost delighted for the new experience.

"You can't blame them," he said with a smile, "I'd be pinching too if someone wanted to use me as bait." Soon we had figured out a way to get their small amounts of meat on the hooks to once again try our luck.

Jesus said, "Can we go a little further, father, this way – to that next bunch of rocks? Somehow I feel we'll have luck there."

There was no harm in humoring the boy, one spot was as likely as another, so we walked over (John ran) to a further outcropping of rocky shore. Before long each of us had caught two fish, of three different types; I caught two small sea-bream, Jesus a gray mullet and a larger bream and John a mullet and a large eel. When he caught his first fish, the mullet, he was crazy with excitement. "Look, mine is bigger than the one Jesus caught, right?" he asked as he held the fish for us to see. "Yes, I'm sure it is," Jesus agreed with his usual kind nature. Then when John caught his eel, he was amazed by the dark, savage looking thing, a large one that must have weighed three pounds, and that writhed and fought so much that John let me take over getting him off the hook, the better for him to jump with happy surprise.

We were keeping our fish in a small, enclosed pool of water convenient to where we were fishing, but I told John I would not include the eel. "That's definitely unclean; we might as well let him back into the sea; we can't eat him."

"Can't keep him? But he's so wonderful. He looks just like a big snake, and did you see he tried to spit blood on you when you removed the hook. Can I have him for a pet at least?" John wanted to know.

"He looks like a snake, but he's a fish, isn't he father?" Jesus asked, though it seemed he already knew the answer.

"That's right. He'll die outside of water before too long. I'm putting him back into the sea."

"But that's not fair. I caught the snake, not you," John yelled, if not with disrespect, at least with some anger.

"Do you want to put him back?" Jesus wondered. "Would that be all right, father?" he asked me.

"Would that make you happy, John?" I asked the boy, who actually had tears in his eyes.

"Keeping him for a pet would make me happy, but I guess since he's a fish, I can't do that. Yes, Cousin Joseph, I guess you're right. But can I hold him for a minute and then let him free?"

John was so volatile. He changed now to a gentle boy, holding the eel, who seemed to not mind, to squirm less once the boy had a hold of him. John petted him softly and walked carefully down from the rocks and then into the water up to his knees before carefully releasing the eel. It never tried to bite him or get away from him, as if it knew he was in loving hands. Of course, he was just a dumb fish, but still it seemed that way.

We continued to have good luck; we caught enough fish, some of a decent size, including a two-pound sea bass. I knew we would have a wonderful dinner of fresh fish at our campfire that evening. When our time was almost up, John asked if we could stop fishing so he could try to swim in the ocean.

"But you don't know how to swim, do you child?" I asked him.

"Is it hard to learn? I bet I can," he assured me.

"Perhaps we can go into the water up to our waists, but no further," I decided. "It's not very often one gets to be in the Lord's great ocean."

I think Jesus would have preferred to keep fishing, but he deferred to his cousin's wishes. The boys removed some of their clothing to be able to be in the water more freely. I stayed a little closer to the shore, a bit worried about someone coming along who might try to steal our supplies; the waves kept lapping up on my feet as if to chide me for my caution. Of course, I was ready to jump in as soon as John tried to get in too deep and I promised him there would be great trouble if he tried. The boys went out together; Jesus sought to hold John's hand but John broke free and splashed in the water, then splashing Jesus. Both boys laughed. They started to stray into deeper water, still with their heads easily above the water line, but I was unfamiliar with how quickly the water might get deeper, so I shouted to them to stray no further. John pretended not to hear me and went deeper; in fact he submerged himself totally in the water over his head, before jumping back up. Just when I was relieved to see his head above water, he grabbed Jesus by the arm and dragged him deeper into the sea. I ran into the water, its heaviness making it difficult to run and the tide working against me. Soon I was almost within reach; John had stopped going further as he heard my approach, but he took Jesus and grabbed him by the top of the head and pushed down, immersing him completely in the water, as if he wanted to drown him. But he held on the whole time and after a few beats, reached him back out of the water, actually lifting him in the air, Jesus splashing down closer to me.

"What are you doing you crazy child?" I shouted at John, but instead of fearing my voice, he ran in the water to where I had grabbed onto Jesus to make sure he was all right.

"Jesus touched the crabs and petted the eel too. He needed a tevilah. What better mikvah than the great sea? Right, Cousin Joseph? You touched it too; you should cleanse yourself too, shouldn't you?"

I didn't know whether to think the boy was mocking me and more importantly the ways of his people, or was instead sincere in his belief that we all needed a ritual cleansing. His eyes were so bright, with mischief, but also with the joy of actually being in the ocean, a lonely boy sharing the adventure of the sea with his cousins. Jesus I saw was not frightened or undone; instead he was smiling and shaking his head to get the water and sand out of his ears. I ran towards John, but instead of hitting him or yelling at him, I grabbed him by the hand, told Jesus to join us, grabbed him by the other, and then, as we went into deeper water still, that I at my height could navigate, I told the children, "One, two three," and we all went under the water together, holding our breath and holding on to each other and then jumping back up above the water, laughing and shaking our heads with joy.

"Are we cleansed enough now, Cousin John?" I asked the boy as I ran us back towards shore.

"Sure, sure we are. Let's go eat some fish now, all right?" he shouted.

"First we have to clean them and cook them," Jesus reminded us.

"Can I help?" John wanted to know.

"Yes, that's a wonderful idea," I responded as I continued to hold the hands of two very special little boys, as if I could hold onto their innocence and youth for them just by not letting go.

Chapter Sixteen

One day, a little after the time of Jesus's eleventh birthday, as I was coming in from my workshop to have lunch, I was surprised to find Jesus and Mary arguing.

"But how can it be wrong, mother, to feed the poor? All of scripture commands us to do so."

"I'm not telling you to ignore the poor, just not to hug lepers. It's certainly not the same thing," Mary said, with more edge in her voice than either Jesus or I was accustomed to. "You can leave food for them where they know to look for it, like others with compassion do, but you mustn't touch them."

"But the poor men and women are suffering from more than hunger. There is spiritual food too, mother, you've told me so yourself." Jesus's tone remained respectful but intent.

"Pity the poor lepers," Mary encouraged, "though, after all, they are suffering because of their own sins or the sins of their ancestors"

"That I cannot believe," Jesus told his mother.

"But the elders tell us this is true and who are you, a child, to question their wisdom?" Mary asked, with a bit of surprise in her tone.

"I don't know, mother, but something in me tells me it can't be true. Most of the lepers seem like good men and women to me, and why would a loving God punish them for something done by their ancestors? It doesn't make sense." Jesus's tone was not dismissive, but rather genuinely confused and centered on his concern for the suffering of the lepers.

"At fault or not, they have a disease that will destroy you if you get too near to them," Mary responded, in a louder voice than I had ever heard her use, resonating with worry and fear. "They know enough to avoid people; they know it's for everyone's welfare. And fair or not, I want you to promise me you'll not hug, nor even touch, a leper ever again, now until forever. You have much to do in your life ahead and you have to make wise choices always."

"Listen to your mother, Jesus, she is only trying to protect you," I offered.

"But who will protect the lepers, father? And who will protect us from our own neglect of their real needs? Mother, your command I obey for now, because you are my mother, but forever is too long a time to be without compassion."

The boy had come often to speak this way, like an adult. Though he showed no miraculous powers or other signs, he certainly knew his scriptures and was becoming more thoughtful and worrisome all the time. He seemed the same happy, healthy boy he had been as a small child when we'd take a trip to the Sea of Galilee to fish, or when he would continue to improve as a craftsman, and could feel my pride in that improvement, but this newer Jesus, who worried over lepers, who seemed sad that his grandfather consorted so often with the Romans in his business dealings, who even questioned me once about the sincerity of a few of the Pharisees who were among our most respected men, this Jesus was becoming more each day the usual one.

I think the shift started when his grandmother died. Anne took ill suddenly, when Jesus was about nine and a half, and the end came quickly, in spite of all of Joachim's money thrown towards her care. Mary felt the need finally to let Anne know all about who Jesus was, how he had come into the world and what he was meant to become; I guess she thought it would make her last moments happier to know she had been the grandmother of the Messiah. She was probably right. The problem was that Anne had the chance to speak to Jesus one last time before she passed, and either in her delirium or in her simple belief that Jesus must already know, she told him, "I knew you were meant for great things. Son of the Most High, you will bring back glory to your people Israel." I know she said these things because Jesus brought them back to me and puzzled over them, expecting me to be as confused by her words as he was. That's the tack I took, telling him they were the disjointed thoughts of a woman undone by her illness and last moments, but probably something about the way I spoke planted doubt in Jesus's mind, and after that moment was when he began to question everything more, and to seem less happy overall.

Mary and I had long ago decided not to tell Jesus anything unless we received a sign from one of the angels or other clear evidence that we should intervene. Still, I was feeling more and more like it wouldn't be right to lie to the boy, if he ever asked me direct questions. And of course Mary was incapable of telling a lie, so I hoped he would not ask her, unless that was what was meant to be.

Things got worse still when he turned eleven and two things were most at fault, my time in Sepphoris and a girl his age, a girl named Martha.

Sepphoris was actually the hometown for Joachim and Anne and Mary's birthplace. But Joachim had decided the place was too volatile and too under Greek and Roman influence for his taste, so he had settled in Nazareth and made his fortune there, though in his later years he was happy to keep in contact with his old town, as it had begun to flourish in the past years under further Roman influence. One day, in fact, he stopped at my workshop, a rare kind of visit from him, so I knew something was up.

"You've done well, my son the craftsman; your skills are now well known throughout Galilee."

He never called me his "son," so I became more suspicious while maintaining a respectful tone.

"Yes, I've been fortunate in many ways," I nodded.

"Word of your skill has spread to the Romans at Sepphoris, and they have asked me to invite you to take part in a grand venture of theirs, which will require the skills of many men."

I stopped what I was doing, put down my saw and chose my words carefully: "I'm happy where I am and though the Romans mostly treated me well in Egypt, I don't long to work for them again, or for anyone but myself."

Joachim did not seem to take offense. Instead, he leaned against a sawhorse and spoke to me as if I were a child needful of instruction.

"What the Romans want they usually get. But they pay well. They are building a great theatre in Sepphoris and need your carpentry skills especially."

"And what is a theatre?" I asked.

"A theatre? Well, you know, a theatre is why, well, what does it matter what it is? Some kind of large structure with seating for hundreds where the Romans perform their rituals, perhaps. I've already told them of your interest; you will start to work there next week."

"How can you promise what I have not agreed to?" I said, losing my respect in both tone and manner towards my greedy old father-in-law. Ever since his wife's death he had thrown himself all the more into his business dealings and now he had thrown me into them too. "And how can you want me to separate myself from my family?"

"What separation? Sepphoris isn't more than an hour's walk northwest of here. And of course to save time you can go back and forth with Sarah, each day, or I'll get you a camel if you'd rather and save you even more time. And there are so many of our own people there that the Romans allow us to honor the Sabbath. They'll pay you well, plus I have made a promise."

I didn't need the money; our needs were simple and the only thing the additional income might support was all the food and clothing we were constantly giving to the poor in our town. Still, I knew Mary would want me to humor her father and I knew the Romans would want me to fulfill the promise Joachim had made. So it was that I was soon working long days in the hot sun of a construction site, helping to frame what would be the largest structure in the town already known as the "Jewel of Galilee."

To me it seemed more like what Sodom must have been like. There were all manner of gentiles there, Greeks, Romans, Parthians, Medes and many others, as well as a number of Jews, many of whom acted more like pagans than the pagans themselves. There were several taverns of the type I had frequented in Egypt, and many of the same sorts of women. These women did not restrict themselves to the taverns, though; one saw them on the streets and marketplaces of the city, playing their harps and inviting men to partake of their pleasures. It was rumored that even some Jewish girls had fallen into the trade, and this of course was most forbidden. Sadly, though, I discovered it was true when more than once a young woman would call out to me in my native tongue, with no trace of the accent that Safiya had had when she spoke poetry to me from our holy books. Still, I resisted, having gotten myself accustomed to a celibate life and not wanting to wander again away from righteousness. But then one day it was as if the devil himself was out courting my disaster and disgrace.

I was walking away from the theatre site, off to ride my borrowed camel back to Nazareth before dark, when I heard a woman's cry. The voice sounded strangely familiar, though at first the words were foreign, though finally the cries for help came out in my own language, but with the accent of a foreigner, perhaps an Egyptian. As I ran to see what the trouble was, I saw a man pulling a woman by her hair as he attempted to hit her with his other hand. She struggled gamely, but he was a big man and very angry.

"You miserable harlot, do you dare to refuse me? This is what you get for your daring, whore."

The man was not a Roman, but one of my own countrymen, a lower worker on the construction crew. "Daniel, what ails you? Leave this woman alone."

"What? Who dares? Oh, it's you, Joseph. This whore won't take credit, though she knows we get paid tomorrow. Can you imagine such a one?"

"She must make her living too. Why not wait until tomorrow, or better still why not find a more willing companion?"

"You're the boss, Joseph. I doubt she'd be much good anyway after the beating I've given her. Tomorrow it is."

I knew the man was only complying in fear of what I might do to his future work chances, since he knew the Romans respected my work and he knew who my father-in-law was. Still, I was glad to have stopped him. My gladness was replaced by shock when I went to help the woman to her feet and saw who I had rescued, Rehema, Safiya's friend from my days in Egypt.

"So, I'm glad to know you are good for something, craftsman," she said as she allowed me to help her up. Her hair was now black as a crow's, but the makeup around her eyes was running down from her sweat and perhaps tears, making those tears seem black as well. "That brute has made me wrench my knee in the struggle. Would you be kind enough to help me back to my humble home?"

"Has Safiya made this journey with you too? Will she be awaiting when we get there?" I asked with a mix of curiosity and fear in my voice, and perhaps longing as well.

"Safiya is dead, craftsman," Rehema told me in a brutal tone. "She took some disease from a Roman pig, and once she was so marked, her career was at an end. I tried to help her as much as I could, but her last days were sad ones. In her memory, Joseph of Nazareth, please help her poor friend."

I didn't know whether Rehema was feigning her severe limp or not. Something about hearing of Safiya's end made me reckless; a woman who would have introduced me to love making, who seemed to have a real and passionate attraction to me, now food for the worms and I still a sad virgin. In the intervening years I had never strayed, but mostly I had kept far away from temptation rather than facing it and turning it away. Holding onto Rehema as I walked her home, this time with no bit of dullness from wine, brought me to a heated state even before we reached her little house, so much like the house that Safiya had lived in back in Cairo. Once we did enter Rehema's room, she directed me to get her to her bed, but then she pulled me down with her upon it. And when she kissed me, full on the lips I was ready to respond, so full of sadness and longing and regret at once. She felt for my privates, which almost seemed to jump at her touch, then laughed and pushed me hard away.

"So you are no eunuch or lover of men after all, craftsman? I had always tried to comfort Safiya by telling her it was so, but instead you were just a fool in refusing her. Well, I refuse you too. Will you now beat me like your countryman? Go ahead, but I still refuse you, hypocrite Jew, for the sake of my lost kinswoman, she who was fool enough to fall for a man like you."

Her words shamed me, angered me, but also allowed my escape. I was not going to force myself on this sad woman, whose figure still was pleasing, but whose face in the lamplight showed her age and all she had suffered at the hands of men. Men like me, I understood. "I apologize to you for my weakness. Your beauty has caused me to act badly," I said as I made my way out of her room.

"Your words cannot excuse you either, Jew," she shouted at me as I fled. "Your longing is only equaled by your hypocrisy."

My shame carried me all the way home, the last two miles in the darkness, where I feared I would be attacked by any one of the number of thieves who frequented this road back from unholy Sepphoris. Instead, the Lord kept me safe, no matter how little I deserved it.

Chapter Seventeen

The more I thought about my close call with Rehema, the less I saw it as a victory over sin. After all, I had been completely ready to give myself over to her; it was she who rejected me, and while I had never been the type who could force myself on a woman, it still remained true that only her refusal had prevented my infidelity. What disarmed me the most was how quickly it had all happened. One moment I was faithful Joseph, the man who was secretly living a life of celibacy though married, the next I was just another overheated patron of a tempting prostitute. If my virtue really was that uncertain, how could I rely on it? The week that followed in Sepphoris I found myself giving the eye to any number of Rehema's co-workers; worse still, I found myself looking with secret and forbidden longing at many of my neighbors' wives and daughters back in Nazareth. I was, after all, still a healthy man in the prime of life; shutting myself off from women was the really unnatural thing. Still, there was Mary, my wholly perfect wife, and deceiving her or hurting her seemed too awful a price to pay to relieve my lust. I tried to settle back, then, as best as I could, into an ever more uneasy chastity and prayed for strength to avoid the temptations of the devil while continuing to avoid the sin of Onan, at least as much as was humanly possible.

Perhaps I would have failed in this resistance had it not been for my having to turn my attention back towards what Jesus himself was going through then, as he suffered the pangs of his own first love and the doubts and guilt and confusion that went with it.

Her name was Martha. She was about the same age as Jesus; she was visiting with the family of her mother's sister in Nazareth; Martha had been left with them to aid her aunt who was recently widowed and in need of some help and support. This Martha was hard-working and very mature for her age, just the kind of person best able to help her aunt through both her grief and the raising of three small children suddenly without their father. Though Martha had little time to herself, Jesus encountered her when he brought food from us to share with the family or when she was out gathering water and she had made quite an impression upon him.

"She's so beautiful, father, with such beautiful, dark eyes full of sympathy. And she works so hard for her aunt and her family; the woman does almost nothing, because she's still so sad and overcome, but Martha does it all without complaint. Sometimes I help her with her tasks and she appreciates my help with such simple gratitude that it makes me want to weep. I want to do everything for her; she is so worthy of being loved."

"Yes, I think I understand how you feel," I told Jesus, as I patted him on the shoulder. "What you're feeling is completely natural. You're a really kind person and so you're always going to be attracted to people who also are good and kind."

"But it's more than that, father," Jesus assured me in that totally sincere and innocent way he had of talking then. We were eating our meagre lunch right in the shop that day, just a few weeks after my stint at Sepphoris had passed. I was trying to catch up on all the work I had had to put off, and Jesus was as ever my faithful helper. In spite of his youth, his skills were already closer to that of a master craftsman than an apprentice. Still it was his youth that was at issue now, as I realized he was in the throes of something stronger than admiration for a nice little girl. "What more is there, my son?" I asked

"I think about Martha all the time. I think about being with her, and though I know I have not yet reached my manhood, I think about wanting to embrace her, to let her know how much I care for her. The thought of her returning to her family in Bethany makes me nervous and sad, even though there has been no talk of her leaving soon. I'm already wondering if we can visit with them when we next go to Jerusalem, even though she hasn't even left Nazareth yet. I don't think I'll be able to stand living a day without seeing her."

The boy was really getting worked up, but I didn't know quite what to tell him so he continued: "Are these feelings normal, father? I'm afraid to tell mother, since so much of what feels natural to me she tells me I must not feel, though she never explains why."

"Your mother is an angel on earth," I responded, "but yes, there are some things it may be better you not share with her. I'm telling you, though, that there's nothing wrong with how you are feeling. Though you are yet a boy, soon you will come into your manhood and I'm happy your attraction is to one who is so modest and kind."

I tried not to see a problem in Jesus feeling this way about a neighbor girl, especially one who was not even a native of our town and might soon be leaving to rejoin her family. Jesus, it seemed, was a normal, healthy child and the feelings he was going through would never lead him astray, I believed, since they were so innocent and pure. Didn't these feelings that a young man has for a woman, especially when so innocently expressed by the boy, come directly from the Most High? Mary, unfortunately, felt very differently about the whole thing.

It was weeks after my conversation with Jesus when Mary asked him to bring a fresh honey cake, which she had learned to make almost as well as those of her cousin Elizabeth, over to his grandfather's house. Jesus gave me an odd sort of almost pleading look before he took the cake and headed out. I wondered why my wife did not think to have all three of us make the visit; I hadn't long to wait to learn why she made that choice.

"What can you be thinking Joseph?" she began. "Jesus has admitted to me that you've known of his feelings for this Martha girl for some time now, yet you didn't share that with me, nor even forbid the boy from these feelings — you've even encouraged them."

Mary was as angry as a perfect person can allow herself to be. Her blue-grey eyes were flashing at me, accusing me, but I did not feel guilty, though neither was I amazed at her attitude.

"What is the harm in the boy feeling affection for such a nice girl as this Martha?"

"Her virtue is not the issue."

"Well, that's a relief," I responded.

"This is not a joke, not at all. Today I caught him hugging the girl, embracing her as she cried over how little her aunt seems to be getting better."

"He was just consoling her, then. He's a very compassionate young man," I said with pride in my voice.

"At his age even an innocent hug can lead, can lead to feelings that might lead to sin. You know who he is. You know we must protect him — how can you not have warned him to avoid all occasion for sin?"

"How can you ask me such a question, woman?" I responded, perhaps now with my own dark eyes flashing. "I've never understood why you and I have to remain apart, yet I've respected your demand. Now are you telling me the boy too must avoid even the most innocent of contact?"

Mary made no reply, but her eyes then had a look that told me I was only at the tip of what she was really trying to tell me.

"You're saying the boy will become a man and also, like you, like me, be forever forbidden to know a loving touch? How can you imagine this child, this innocent, loving child, would ever find occasion for sin in his love for a worthy woman?"

"It cannot be. He is destined for greatness; he is to be the King of Kings. Don't pretend not to remember. He can never know a normal marriage."

"You mean like ours?" I interrupted with more anger, an anger that was resurrecting with every word my spouse hurled at me.

"I mean no marriage at all, not even like ours. He must be for all the people and can never devote himself to any one person as a husband must for his spouse. We have to start teaching him now. He should not fall for even the most virtuous of girls, since he is not allowed to fall. You have to have a talk with him; he listens to me and obeys me, but he doesn't understand. I've forbidden him to see Martha again, and he will obey me, but he is so upset I'm afraid for him. You have to explain to him why this must be so."

"Don't tell me what I have to do. I'm so tired of you telling me how to behave." I began, more upset than I had been in years. "I can't explain what I don't understand myself. I will not forbid him to see this girl. They're just children and he hasn't done anything wrong."

"No, not intentionally of course, but still we must…"

"We must what? And why must we?" I interrupted. "I thought Jesus was the son of the Most High, the very one who insists we love our neighbors as ourselves. I thought he came to save his people Israel. Yet you tell him not to hug the lepers, not to hug a crying child. Where is the love he has come into the world to share? Where is the love? Isn't it better to sin with the possibility of love alive than to remain a saint who can touch no one?"

Mary looked at me. She said nothing. She started actually to shake with what I at first thought was more anger, but which I soon realized was great sadness. Tears filled her beautiful eyes and she shook more till I thought she would have to fall to the floor. Finally she said, between tears and gasps for air: "My husband, my love, I am not such a monster. I have longed to ease your pain, I have longed to have a normal life too, but I am as ever the handmaiden of the Most High. Whatever I do, whatever I ask of you, whatever I will ask of Jesus is done from love, but a love that has to be of the spirit and not of the flesh. Please understand. Please help me. Please forgive the life I called you to when I chose you for my spouse. Please help the child begin to understand who he has to be."

Her words, her gestures, might have just made me angrier still, but the Lord knew the man he had chosen; her honest sadness moved me almost to tears myself. I touched her lightly first on one shoulder, than when she didn't repel me, I held her hand. Finally, I embraced her, in a hug she knew was all spirit and sympathy and so one she could accept, as a person who has lost a loved one accepts the embrace of a sympathizer.

"I will talk to the boy," I promised her. Though I did not look forward to the conversation, I understood that it had to happen. Jesus was not destined any more than I was, any more than his poor mother was, to a normal, much less a happy life on this earth.

Chapter Eighteen

I compromised with Jesus. I told him it was fine to be friends with Martha but to remember that a proper Jewish man or even a boy who was close to his manhood had to keep a respectful distance from any woman. A month later Martha went back to her family in Bethany and though Jesus was very upset about it for weeks after, I told him he had to accept the ways of our Lord, and though he seemed every week a little more inward, less the happy child I had grown to love, he still respected and obeyed his parents. He put perhaps even more effort and purpose into his work in the shop. By age twelve he was almost as skilled as I and he seemed to enjoy the work, particularly when it involved some problem solving or creativity. He had grown strong from this work with wood and stone and metal, and he also grew tall, almost as tall as I, and I have always been considered a tall man. People spoke even more of how we resembled each other, and their comments made me proud, since I too was willing to believe something of the best person I could be was reflected in young Jesus.

Maybe it was the nightmares that took away our last days of peace or maybe it was just the very passage of time. Jesus was getting ready to take on the responsibilities of a Jewish adult, the Yom Kippur fast and other rites and responsibilities that went with being a grown up. His knowledge of Torah and of our traditions was extraordinary in one so young, but getting ready for manhood was not just a matter of praying or knowing scripture and law. One evening he came to me before it was time to go to sleep for the night; his mother was in prayer in a farther room; he seemed to have waited for her to be away to come to me.

"Father, I am afraid to sleep. The past weeks I've been having really awful dreams, and they keep repeating themselves."

Jesus did not seem frightened as much as he seemed genuinely sad and burdened by what he was about to describe. I said nothing, but motioned to him that we should both sit down on the divan we had recently put together in the shop from Jesus's own design. I then waited for him to say more.

"Each night I find myself surrounded by strange creatures – men who are naked and have tails like serpents' bodies. They tell me I will suffer for nothing, since they cannot be defeated. They tell me 'Your father sent you to suffer and die.' No father who loves his son would ask him to die the horrible death that awaits you."

"Always these same words, my son?" I asked, saddened myself to hear what he had been going through and longing to tell him that he had great triumph, not suffering ahead, since he was to be the Messiah. Of course, I too remembered the words of Shlomo, a prediction he made right before insisting we leave for Egypt, 'He'll cause almost as much misery as joy for thousands of years to come', but I knew this was no time to share those angelic predictions with my frightened son.

"Always something similar. But last night was the worst of all. One of the demons, with the face of an angel except for the fire that seemed to glow from his orange eyes, took me in hand even as he suddenly grew wings, dark, powerful wings he used to lift us both in the air to fly us to a mountain top. There we looked down on strange scenes of people who dressed nothing like us, men and women of different nations, and, according to this demon of different times. As we looked closer we saw they were killing each other in battle and worse were scenes of merciless torture that some were inflicting on those they seemed to hate with all their hearts. And the demon told me, 'Listen, Jesus, they are doing these evil deeds in your name. They will be called Crusaders, Inquisitionists, and other strange titles, but they will share this bloodlust for murder and torture, all done in the name of Jesus.'"

"I turned away, unable to tolerate these scenes, but the demon had control of what I saw, and next he took me to the most horrid scene of all, thousands and thousands of people starving to death, suffering to the point of being living skeletons, then being herded into strange buildings where their final end came in smoke and fire. These people I felt the most sadness and pity for but I was helpless to aid them. And then the demon said: 'Mark this scene well, Jesus. These are your own people, the people of Israel; millions of them will die, not just in this scene I show to you, but all through the intervening years, die from the hate and cruelty of your many followers. Die in your name. Die because your father has sent you here so you too may suffer and die.'"

Jesus recited the words from his dreams with so much sad conviction that I knew he had suffered every second of each dream's reality. I drew him to myself and tried to reassure him.

"These are just crazy nightmares. How could any of that be true? How would the Most High allow these awful things your dreams have predicted ever to happen? How could the God of Abraham, the God of Moses and God of David ever allow his people to suffer so? And how could you, still a child, be responsible for any of it?" Of course, as I posed these questions to Jesus I was wrestling with them myself, still unable to conceive of so much horror ahead for the very Son of God.

"But the demon insisted my father brought me into this world to suffer and die. I know you love me, father, but it all seemed so real, but I know you love me, father."

"Yes, of course – that you will always be able to rely on. Feel my hands upon you, son. These hands are human hands. These hands are real hands. No cloudy dream will ever replace them. No number of dream demons will ever stop me from protecting you from harm." Of course I knew which father this dream demon was really talking about, but that truth I also kept to myself.

Jesus seemed somewhat reassured, but the dreams continued; in fact they only got worse. His cries at night were not for help for himself, but rather in sympathy for all the people he saw suffering. Mary finally got the truth out from him when she insisted we go into his room to check on him. She had me sleep by his side that night, but the next morning she insisted we finally have the talk we had been putting off. She took the nightmares as the sign we had been awaiting, from demons rather than angels, but still a sure sign.

And so we told him everything. How an angel had told Mary she would receive the son of the Most High as her child, straight from the Holy Spirit, with no mortal man necessary. How I had been visited too by an angel to assure me of Mary's virtue and of my own role in raising this boy who was to be the Messiah of his people. We told him of what Elizabeth had said upon our visit to her during Mary's pregnancy, what the shepherds and the Magi had proclaimed, the warnings of the old priest and priestess in the temple about Jesus's future and our own. We explained to him why we had kept these things a secret not only from him but from everyone, with the exception of his grandmother Anne and only on her death bed, and how we had had no other word from our Lord on how things would proceed, but knew we were to raise the son of the Most High as our own. Mary and I took turns explaining things to the boy, and he looked at us with eyes, his mother's eyes, that were deep with wonder but also with something else I cannot really explain. It was almost as if this talk of the Holy Spirit had kindled the spirit in the boy's own eyes. But one might have also have taken the look instead for despair.

"How can this be?" were his first words. "Everyone says how much we look alike. Surely, I am your son, father. Surely, this cannot be."

Jesus said these words without conviction, knowing of course we would have no motive to tell him such an awful, awesome lie, but still he clung to his disbelief, like a more hopeful kind of dream.

"Joseph the craftsman is who your heavenly father has ordained to protect you and help you grow," Mary said.

"But he is not my real father," the boy mused. "And all these years you have acted the part of a father, made me obey and listen to you, when really, all along, you know it was a lie."

"The Most High ordained It to be so," Mary explained.

"The Most High, you said yourself, has told you nothing since my birth. You chose to keep this incredible secret from me. Now when I am besieged by demons, where is this father to help me? Instead, I learn that I have no father on earth, and hear from demons each night how my 'father' seeks only my suffering and destruction."

Jesus said these last words with anger and then raced from the room. I was going to chase after him, but Mary told me to leave him be. I thought for a time that he had run away from home, as he wasn't there all day to help me with our work. However, at dinner time he reappeared, though he spoke only when spoken to. The next day, though, he was back to work with me, and showed no signs of disrespect, nor did he ask any questions. When Mary tried speaking further with him at meal time, he only said, "I know what you tell me is true, mother, most blessed mother, but I don't know what it means yet any more than you."

Jesus became more somber and quiet; respectfully passed on my idea for a fishing trip, did his work but without seeming to enjoy it. Then it was time for one of our annual treks to the temple in Jerusalem, this time for the Passover celebrations. Joachim, too old to make the trip himself anymore, arranged for us to be part of a large caravan of worshippers headed that way. We arrived without real incident and took part in the ceremonies and observances, which Jesus could now more fully partake in and appreciate, though he seemed to show no especial enthusiasm for any of it. Before we knew it, it was time to head back to Nazareth. I traveled with the men; Jesus told me he wanted to spend the time with his mother instead and it was really the last year when that would be an option for him, before his full manhood at age thirteen, so I agreed. We traveled a full day before we made ready to make camp for the night. Eventually I came to where Mary was staying with the other women. After a few moments I asked: "Is Jesus resting already in that tent that was just set up?"

"Why do you ask me, husband? I haven't seen the boy since we left Jerusalem."

"What are you talking about? He told me he was going to spend the day with you."

"But I tell you I haven't seen him," Mary said, with a sudden look of alarm filling her eyes.

Of course we spent the next minutes searching all through the caravan's camp for our son. He was not anywhere among us. We had made a full day's journey away from Jerusalem only to realize we had made it without Jesus. The caravan leaders would not of course agree to head back, but a few of Mary's cousins convinced them to loan us a camel, and since all knew we were of Joachim's family, they also made sure we had provisions for the trek back to Jerusalem and eventually to Nazareth again.

The next few days were awful as we first made our way back alone to the holy city and then as we searched without luck for Jesus in that city. We assumed he had awaited this opportunity to run away and we feared that by now he might have joined some other caravan headed to only the Most High knew where. Oddly, rather than being angry with each other, Mary and I supported each other in our pain and worry and prayed together for the boy's safety. Finally, about to give up, Mary suggested we go back to the temple to pray. Our amazement was great when we found Jesus speaking with a number of priests and scribes within one of the temple courtyards. We approached with more trepidation than the parents of a twelve-year-old runaway might have had in normal circumstances, but we could hear Jesus almost holding court, speaking with confidence and perhaps even some pride, about holy matters. The men who he spoke with seemed impressed by his knowledge and his confidence. We waited for a break in their conversation, as it seemed somehow a sacrilege to interrupt any sooner.

"Jesus," his mother began. "Why have you left us without a word? We've spent the last few days searching for you all over Jerusalem. Your father and I have been beside ourselves with worry and grief. Why would you do such a thing?"

Jesus looked at us and seemed like he would say nothing. But then he got up from where he had been sitting and looked his mother in the eye before saying, "Why were you two searching for me? Didn't you know that I had to be in my father's house?"

The way Jesus said father was almost enough to break me. I knew exactly which father he was talking about and that he was finally acting out over what we had laid upon him a few months before. It seemed impossible that this could be the same happy child I had grown so to love. He seemed instead a new person, a new man, and one who knew who he was by knowing now who I really was.

"You will come home with us now," Mary said. "You are to obey us and no longer give us cause for alarm. We all have to do what the Most High ordains and he has given you two parents to obey."

Jesus did not protest. He also did not apologize. He came back with us and gave us no further trouble. A few weeks later when I asked him about the bad dreams he told me, "My nightmares have ended." I believed him, but we both knew that really they had only just begun.

Chapter Nineteen

The next few years were really difficult for all three of us. Jesus did his work in the shop dutifully but without enthusiasm or artistry. Whatever Mary or I asked him to do, he would do, but he did most everything in a somber, joyless way. He spent most of his spare time in prayer and in scriptural study, but he did not seek to talk to me about what he was reading the way he once did. More than once I confronted him in the shop, asking him if he understood that with his special status came special responsibility and that moping or being upset with his parents were not really options for the son of the Most High. Once he answered me, "If I'm meant for great things, surely they won't happen here and surely not while I am so young. Being so young, I cannot yet leave to where I am destined and I don't know where that might be anyway. And though I pray without ceasing to my heavenly father, as yet I've received no response. No angel has visited me, only dream demons with their awful lies, and even they have stopped their visits. What would you have me do, my earthly father?"

What would I have him do? I'd have him be an obedient son, but he was already doing that. I'd have him try to find joy in the blessings bestowed upon us by the Most High, but how could I sell that option when I myself was fairly joyless, with a wife I could not embrace, work that was more difficult than rewarding now that my son knew he was not my son, a father-in-law who pretty much ran the town and still had no genuine respect for me, and a future that I did not understand, since there were no visiting angels available anymore to explain it all to me either. What would it mean for Jesus to be the Messiah? I had no idea, nor did Mary, so how could we explain it to Jesus? So he continued to brood and we continued to be far less happy than the earthly parents of the Son of God would ever have been expected to be.

The change came during one of our visits to Jerusalem, which we continued to combine with a visit to John and Elizabeth. John already had a beard and his hair was as wild as ever. He also was as active and talkative and what I might call half-crazy as ever, and at first Jesus seemed less willing to tolerate his ways than ever. Really his disinclination for his cousin had been growing with every visit we made.

It seemed as though John wanted something from him but would not say what it was, or that he knew something that he wanted to tell us but could not. Jesus remained polite but declined to go on walks with John unless his mother insisted. To his cousin's suggestion that we redo our fishing trip to the great sea he flatly responded, "I don't fish anymore." It was true, we hadn't gone fishing together since he had discovered his true parentage and it was one of his most direct reactions against me that he could take without seeming to have done anything wrong. Not everyone likes to fish, after all.

It was the evening before we were to leave for Jerusalem and John had not returned from one of his nature walks. His lateness was not unusual but after a few more hours had passed from his expected return, we all began to worry, but particularly his mother Elizabeth. "He seemed more frantic than ever before he left," Elizabeth told us; I had to take her word for that, since she lived with the wild young man every day. Still, I was worried for his welfare too, and took a lantern and prepared to search for the boy. Mary told Jesus, "Go with your father, so you can help to find your cousin." Ever obedient, Jesus asked for a second lantern and we were on our way in the dark together.

The road to Elizabeth's little house was not much of a road at all and the area all around was hilly. We guessed we would not be so lucky as to see John returning towards us on that road, though I hesitated to venture into the hills in such darkness. Jesus walked along with me silently, and that silence became intolerable as we walked aimlessly along the rutted road.

"Should we go into these hills? We have no weapon to protect us against animals, and the way is uncertain," I pointed out.

"The way is always uncertain, my earthly father. One must trust always in the Lord, isn't that so?"

There was no mockery in Jesus's voice, though the words themselves could have been taken for sarcasm. I chose instead to ignore that possibility.

"You're right, my son. All we have in this vast darkness is our trust that our Lord will not lead us astray, is a loving father who demands our trust through every trial, even as he tested Abraham's faith through his son Isaac. We will go and fear no evil."

I saw Jesus nod his agreement by the light of his lantern and I made ready to walk into the hilly terrain to our left.

"Do you think we should split up and search in two directions for my lost cousin? If we go one way only we might miss him," Jesus said.

"Two together are always better than one," I responded. "Come with me, son, and trust in your father."

I thought I saw a wan sort of smile on his face, but the darkness made that uncertain. He followed me though and we approached the dark together. We called out, "John, John," again and again, but received no answer. We walked on and on, getting further and further from the road, climbing hills, stumbling more than once and all the while calling out, with no idea as to whether we were anywhere near where John might be. I was about to tell Jesus that we should turn back towards the road, hoping that maybe John, so accustomed to this land as we were not, would have already made it back to his house by another way. But then Jesus spoke. "Do you hear him, father? Do you hear the cry of my cousin John?"

At first I heard nothing, except maybe a jackal's call, but then, yes, I heard a voice, calling out not in pain or worry, but almost with what I would call ecstasy, if I really knew what that call might be like. We walked towards the voice and as we got nearer the words, repeated over and over like a prayer or chant, were familiar: "A voice cries out in the Wilderness, prepare the way of the Lord. Make straight the desert, a highway for our God." John's voice itself became a highway for us, as we followed it to where he was standing on a big boulder, calling out these words of the prophet Isaiah again and again into the great darkness. What happened next surprised me, since Jesus had seemed to want to ignore the insistence and fervor of his cousin over our last several visits. Still, these past few years Jesus had to have been coming into some deep and awesome awareness of his destiny and his future power, so that John's cry must have finally seemed to him as irresistible as it was inevitable. And so Jesus did not reject the call or complain about his crazy cousin's eccentric actions. Instead, Jesus took up the next words from the prophet: "Every valley will be lifted up, every mountain and hill made low. The rough ground will be a plain and the rugged terrain smooth. The glory of the Lord will be revealed and all flesh will see it together. For the mouth of the Lord has spoken."

John's eyes, when we got close enough with our lanterns to see them, were shining with tears and wild fervor. He came down from his rock and kneeled down to Jesus, who lifted him up in an embrace. Both boys then came to me and each took me by one of my hands and Jesus said to me. "Come, father, let us return. Your trust in the Lord has borne great fruit."

As I held the hands of these two boys, each on the threshold of manhood, each full of a fire I could never fully comprehend, I felt almost as if I myself were on fire, but with a fire that burned without consuming or harming. I recognized that my son had been given back to me, given back to me by his crazy cousin who knew somehow fully who Jesus was and who had now revealed it to us both. Jesus was not just the Son of the Most High, he was not just the Messiah to be. Somehow, Jesus was both totally human, through his mother Mary, and totally divine, through the Holy Spirit. And I, Joseph, son of Jacob, a poor craftsman, was the earthly father of a completely human, and wholly divine young man.

Chapter Twenty

Jesus took on the incredible fact that he was a real person but also somehow at once the Lord of Hosts with bravery and good will, but we both knew it was not going to be easy. His mother agreed. The three of us sat together and talked it out; she claimed she had not known for certain but had always suspected that the Son of the Most High had to be at least as much God as he was man, but she still could not comprehend the idea that Jesus was in some sense also our very Lord. It was beyond my comprehension too, but not my belief. I had felt it there, with lightning certainty, on a dark hillside a few miles from Jerusalem. As for Jesus, he had none of the incredible or limitless powers one would expect the Lord to have, but he began to expect when he was fully into his manhood he would have whatever power he needed. Meanwhile, though, being even more certain of the responsibilities that came with his divinity, his human life grew more difficult by the day.

When he was a little past seventeen, two people made his life extremely difficult, though in two very different ways. Altir, the butcher's son, came to be a merciless critic, even while Martha, his first love, made his life even more difficult by the simple act of loving him.

A young unmarried Jew who is keeping to the law of his people does not have much in the way of interaction with women. Jesus, particularly, since he had been told by his mother that he could never marry, should have been even more reticent. Jesus, though, seemed almost to prefer the company of women, always looking to help them carry their water jugs or lighten their load in some other way. And his mother did not question these actions, even if it involved helping an unmarried woman, since she knew he was beyond doing anything inappropriate. Her attitude changed, though, when Martha came back into our lives.

There was nothing extraordinary about Martha in terms of her appearance. She might have been described as almost plain, and one always found her working dutifully whenever she was outside her aunt's house, and within those walls she worked all the more. But Jesus was just as taken by her as ever, and Martha, Mary feared, might start misunderstanding his attentions to her. She came from a good family, one that might not be reticent to align itself with the grandson of the richest man in Nazareth and one of the richest in all of Galilee. Certainly for normal families it would have been a logical connection, especially since the two young people seemed so taken with each other. But, of course, ours was hardly a normal family.

"How can you be so careless of a girl you claim to favor so?" Mary asked Jesus one evening at our supper table. "You know you must follow the law; you are he who has come to fulfill the law, and so you cannot show special favor to one woman. This, of course, Martha will not understand, and it isn't fair of you to place her hopes in a hopeless dream."

"Our son has done nothing wrong. It can't be wrong to care for someone as purely and completely as he cares for Martha," I argued.

"Let him speak for himself," Mary answered me with an almost harsh look. "Son, knowing who you are, how can you let this girl hope you might be available to her in ways you cannot be?"

"Mother, I understand. But as much as I have to feel and anticipate my destiny, I too feel and am human. I've kept my love for Martha pure, without lust, without longing for anything but her happiness. And I feel a sympathy with her and with all women who labor without complaint, who seek after righteousness as much as any man might. And I'm not sure yet if I've really come to fulfill the old laws only. Perhaps some new law, some new way of life will be revealed to me by my father."

"For a young man, even the purest of women could be an occasion for sin," my virgin wife reminded Jesus.

"For others, perhaps, but not for me," Jesus calmly replied. "The one gift I know I've been given by the Most High is the purity of my love for all. You need not worry on that account, mother."

Jesus and I had spoken of this more than once. I had wondered if he would be immune to normal human desire, since he was of God, and not like those Roman gods I had learned of during my time in Egypt and Sepphoris, who mated with humans whenever their own lusts called them to. Jesus had assured me though he had normal human functions that had to be relieved, he never once was close to sin during those times. "Whenever I feel so full of the Lord's urge to be part of going forth to multiply, the great procreant urge of the world, I allow myself to think only of a cosmic love, a natural love that makes all things beautiful or in other words, as they really are, and so my dreams never turn to anything that is not part of the love of both God and neighbor that is our highest calling."

I understood that entirely, since I had tried to push back my own lust, not always as successfully as Jesus had, but then, I was not only wholly but only human. And the more I had been successful the more I had found sympathy with Mary in place of my earlier anger and frustration. Knowing now who our son was and understanding that the role and rise of the people's Messiah was not to be anything like most people expected (though exactly what it would be, we had still no answer to) we were becoming closer to being a family wholly in synch with each other. But Mary still worried about Jesus's love for Martha. And she was after all right to worry, as it turned out.

One evening we were visited by Martha's father, who had come all the way from Bethany to speak with us. He was a serious and even somber man, with searching, deep brown eyes, and a beard so neat it almost seemed painted on. He had come in his best clothes and with his intentions clear. Clearly he wanted to know our son's intentions.

As he sat at our table, where he partook of some of Joachim's best wine, he waited until Jesus had removed himself before proceeding with his talk; Mary insisted on staying, though it was not the norm. Already, then, Martha's father was forewarned of something unusual.

"It's come to my attention that your son Jesus favors my daughter Martha greatly. Certainly, the time has come for her to consider a life mate. Though I would have preferred to have her marry in Bethany, her time here has made her comfortable with your little town and I'm told Jesus is as skilled a craftsman now as even his father, who has a reputation for excellence throughout Galilee. I know, then, she will never starve. I seek then what is right and I hope you will consider this match a way of uniting our families."

Before Abram, Martha's father, could begin to get to more specific terms of the alliance, Mary intervened.

"I have stayed for this conversation because of our son's unique situation. He has promised his life to the Most High, and will never take a spouse."

"I have heard of Jesus's knowledge of the holy books and this has only made him seem to me a more perfect match for my daughter, who also is a lover of scripture, though a woman. There is no law I know of that takes a priest, scribe or rabbi away from his proper part in raising a family."

"Yes, that's true," I nodded, as I poured Abram more wine, "but Jesus is a special case. He will never marry."

Abram pushed his cup of wine away. "A man who never marries is not wholly a man. Surely, you are not being frank with me, but instead are excusing your son for his advances on my daughter's honor, even while you have some richer match in mind."

"My son has made advances on no one," Mary responded, though she glanced at me with an "I told you this would happen" look that was unmistakable in its accuracy.

"Nothing physical, of course, or I would be angrier still, but certainly he has led my daughter to believe he favors her beyond all others." Abram nearly shouted these words. Our house was small and apparently Jesus had not gone outside, since he came back into the room and responded.

"What you say is true," he said directly to the angry father. "Martha has been, since we were both children, a person who touches me deeply with her simple, loving willingness to serve. She is loving and nurturing with her nieces and nephews, and she is patient and caring for your sister, who you must know is not an easy woman to please. My sympathy and affection for her is beyond love; she makes me know the universe is made for caring and devotion and kindness. But my parents are right, I will never marry, though it grieves me that I will never know that kind of love with someone as wonderful as Martha."

I thought Jesus's speech was beautiful and it spoke so closely to what I had finally come to feel about my life with Mary, with whom I had had to live without physical love, but who certainly was as deserving of love as young Martha. Abram, however, was not impressed.

"You let this young man speak to me, speak for your family," he addressed me harshly. "I can see this is a family that does not know the law it claims so to respect. I can see my daughter is well rid of you all. I forbid your son to see my daughter again."

"You should not speak such words of disrespect to me within my own walls," I told him, though trying to keep my own temper in check.

"You needn't worry, craftsman, I am leaving," he said as he arose from the table. "And my daughter soon will go back to Bethany with me; my sister can look to her own children now for support; I won't endanger my daughter further. But I will tell her of your son's strange ways so she will know what might have befallen her had I not arrived in time."

We were all insulted, as he meant us to be, but we offered no more words since they would have served no purpose. Mary had been right and Jesus understood now why she had wanted him to be more careful. And his sadness over being forbidden to see Martha again was not the only suffering left to him over his mistake.

Altir, son of the local butcher, had never liked Jesus. He was a rough, even crude young man now, but even when they were boys he had been rough and crude and always deriding Jesus for his kindness or, as Altir called it, his "softness." Though Jesus had tried to avoid confrontations with him and had seldom cause to see him (I made trips to the butcher myself and neither Altir nor his father ever said a harsh word to me), he still ran into him from time to time and Altir would mock him, and Jesus would never say anything harsh in reply. Somehow, though, Jesus's time with Martha was of interest to the butcher's son, perhaps because he himself had favored her. That was my guess at least to explain what happened.

I was outside our shop looking over some lumber that had just been delivered, when I saw Altir enter our work place; he did not see me. Jesus was inside working with the artful diligence that had rekindled after our experience in the hills with his cousin John, but Altir left the door swung open, so I heard every word he shouted.

"So, this is Jesus, son of Joseph, one who favors women but never wants to be with one, ever. I always wanted to see what a eunuch looked like at work, so I came to get a look."

I thought to rush inside. Though I'm not as strong as in my youthful prime, I was still more than a match for this butcher's son, but I thought I'd wait to see how Jesus would handle this roughneck, since he'd probably become more and more misunderstood as the years ahead came upon us.

"I am no eunuch, Altir, though even the eunuch is worthy of sympathy."

"Yes, and the leper, and the widow and even the tax collector who serves the Romans, thereby serving your grandfather, who sleeps with them."

With these harsh words Altir picked up a two by four with which to menace my son. Still, I hesitated to interrupt. Jesus had a hammer in his hand, after all, and knew well how to swing it.

"My grandfather is a widower and sleeps alone," he responded, "and if you mean to get me angry enough to fight with you, it cannot work and I have no insults to trade back with you, though I'll have to defend myself if you seek to hit me with that wood, since I cannot have you damaging our stock on my hard head, plus my time has not yet come."

Jesus did not exactly stare Altir down. Rather he looked at him with all the power of those blue-grey eyes his mother had blessed him with, showing no fear, no anger and no retreat. When Altir seemed surprised into silence, Jesus added, as he put down his hammer on the work bench: "I made a mistake in my approach to Martha, though my intent and behavior were pure. I applaud you if you have come out of regard for her, but no insults or blows you could offer would make me feel any worse than I already do for having given her any cause for sadness."

Altir again said nothing. I coughed a warning that I was approaching from behind him, and then said: "Altir, how are you this fine morning? Is there anything you need from us or is this a social call only?"

"I just had something I needed to say to your son. I'll be on my way now, thank you." All the anger seemed drained from him, but he had nothing yet within him to take its place and so he left us empty and without another word.

From that day forward Jesus had no trouble with the butcher's son.

Chapter Twenty-One

For the next several years my relationship with both my son and my wife could hardly have been better, given how difficult it always had to be. I had grown accustomed finally to the celibate life, and though Mary grew more beautiful with the years, her holiness became ever more her most prominent feature, and her continued kindness and concern helped me get fully in touch with what I now believed was my purpose in life: to help Jesus find his way. Though I still worked hard at my job and though Mary still lived the hard life of the wife of a craftsman, always doing more than her share of whatever work needed to be done, we often took time as a family to talk over what it was that Jesus would be headed for once he knew it really was his time to venture forth into the larger world.

We were having dinner together after a particularly long day of work. Our dinner that night was very ordinary: bread, wine, some beans and some goat cheese, and figs for dessert. What was unusual was that Jesus had insisted on helping his mother with its preparation, including the grinding of the wheat to help make it into flour for our bread. This was woman's work, of course; Jesus and I worked long hours each day in our shop and were not expected to help with most domestic tasks. But Jesus more and more had his own ideas about what should and should not be.

"There is something wonderful in preparing the food for our table," he said, "but that wonder lessens when it is all put upon one person. All honest labor is good for the soul, the soul of a woman as well as a man."

"But we spend all day working with a schedule that keeps us at our tasks without time for other work," I reasoned with him. "If you take time away from making the things our customers have ordered, they won't have them when we promised and that's not good business or being a good neighbor."

"That's right, my son," Mary agreed. "I appreciate any time you spend with me, but I am still strong enough to do all the work of the household and happy to do so."

"Mother, you provide us always with a clean and healthy home and plentiful good food to eat. But you also know the holy books as thoroughly as any priest or rabbi and you obey the law of our people with both knowledge and joy. I just want to remind you sometimes that I understand you have been put on this earth to do more than make bread or mend our garments."

"Women have always had their place and it is a good place. A man must love and protect his wife and daughters. There is no shame in making bread or mending a garment," I reasoned.

"And that reminds me that cloak you're wearing is looking pretty ragged, my husband," Mary chided. "You'd better give it to me before you go to sleep tonight."

Jesus smiled rather than taking offense. But still he continued. "Men are hardheaded and set in their ways," he explained. "I see a new order in which there would be nothing surprising in a woman being a scholar or a man learning how to cook or prepare food. But I know the people will not respond well now to these notions, the women as well as the men."

"Hasn't the Lord made men stronger so that they can plow or wield a hammer or slaughter an animal when needed?" I asked. "Aren't we doing as the Lord would have us do?"

Mary passed me the figs; though I hadn't asked for them, I was happy to take them from her. "I think Jesus just wants us to know the Lord loves his daughters equally as well as his sons," she said. "And that a woman is as pleasing to our Lord as any man because she is his daughter, whom he loves as well as his son."

"Yes, mother, you've got it," Jesus smiled again. "And tonight I wanted to help his daughter to make the bread. And any man should be pleased to share the work of the woman and honor both it and her."

This was our son, the young man who continued to minister to the lepers, to feed the poor, the young man who had sympathy even for the prostitutes, tax collectors and other sinners. It seemed there was no one beyond his affection, though he did seem to get angry at those who had the most and shared it least or who made a big show of when they did give charity. His own grandfather he caused to be far more generous with his neighbors than he ever had been before. Time Joachim spent with Jesus helped to transform him, in his last years, into a man who understood there were things far more pleasing to the Most High than sacrificing an ox or following the law to the letter. To my amazement, I watched him join

Jesus on his trips to visit the needy, trips I also took whenever I could find time away from our work. Though some derided us for our generosity, once Joachim was largely behind it, they had to respect what Jesus was trying to accomplish. And though some of the poor seemed to me ungrateful and perhaps even lazy, the ones who really needed his help most I could see loved him as if he were their own son taking care of them in their need. And the children he helped, well, they loved him best of all, as he spent time with them, telling them stories and bringing them little presents, mostly toys he had constructed for them in our shop after hours, little wooden dogs and birds and locusts even, which the children loved to receive. They were so artfully constructed they seemed as if they could come to life if he only asked them to.

I remember one story he shared with a group of children when both Joachim and I were along for the visit. "There was a man who had three sons. This man had great riches and a large, prosperous farm but his wife and his sons were dearer to him than all his money and possessions. And all three sons seemed to love their father as much as he loved them. But then the man suffered great misfortune. His wife grew sick and weak and needed constant care, though the doctors could not cure her. A great drought gripped the land and destroyed all the man's crops. Thieves came in the night and stole many of the man's possessions, including almost all of his stored gold. The man trusted a friend with some of his remaining money, in hopes of regaining some of his fortune, but the friend deceived him and all that money also was lost. Soon he had not even enough wealth to take care of his family as he had before, so he gave each of his sons a small sum he had held back for them and told them they must seek their own fortunes, as they were all of age to go out into the world. The eldest son invested his money wisely and soon bought land with that money and prospered greatly, marrying well so as to increase his fortune. The second son joined a great army and showing well his bravery and skill, rose in the ranks of command to a place of prominence. The youngest son apprenticed to a craftsman and worked hard, but the craftsman was himself a poor man with many small children to feed and so the young man could not ask for a salary such as he might have deserved, preferring to help the good man and his wife as he could by increasing their business through his honest labor."

"Years passed, the mother of the three sons was close to death and the father himself grew weak with grief. The eldest son, hearing of his mother's illness and his father's continuing misfortune sent him some money from his vast holdings. The middle son sent him a small box with a note inside: 'Father, I send you a rare jewel, part of the bounty of our last raid in a foreign land. You can restore yourself to wealth by selling it.' The mother died. The two older sons sent their regrets and apologies for not attending her funeral, since they lived far off and had no time to spare. The youngest son, he reappeared at the house of his father in time to share his father's grief at his house, a house now in sad disrepair with no servants to attend to the father. The young apprentice upon learning of what his brothers had sent said to his father: 'I have no wealth I can give you as my brothers have given; all I can give you is my love, my father. Won't you come and stay with me? My house is little more than a hut, but I have honest work, and every little thing I have will be yours equally.'"

"The father smiled with joy at the return of his youngest son. He took the gifts of his two other children and gave them to the poor; having known poverty himself he was now in sympathy with their plight. Since he himself was no longer poor; he could well afford to be generous."

The story seemed to be concluded, but some of the boys seemed confused: "But how was he not still poor, especially if he gave away the money and the jewel?" one of the children asked.

"Yes, his youngest son had almost nothing," another pointed out.

"He had his son's love and a home with that son," the youngest of all the children, a child of only six or seven, explained. "Always the father had loved his family more than any gold. Isn't that right, teacher?" he asked my son.

"From the smallest mouth comes the biggest truth," Jesus said, and then patted the boy on his head. "As you love one another, so will you be rich, if not in this land, still in the eyes of your heavenly father."

"This is a lesson well worth learning," Joachim said to all the children gathered. "And it's never too early to start learning it, nor too late either."

Joachim was now a man transformed. His gifts to the poor became more and more substantial and given with more and more blessings and gratitude. No one could understand or explain this transformation in the town's once richest man. He gave away so much of what he possessed that he lost that title. And yet he had become richer than ever. This, I believe, was my son's first miracle.

Chapter Twenty-Two

Even as Jesus grew into an adult and became more and more spiritual and concerned with what his role might be in the world, he never gave up his love of fishing. But I never imagined how important fishing and fishermen would become in his life.

I could see he was growing a bit discontent continuing to work as a craftsman. When he reached the age of twenty-three he had a secure living from our work and people in town expected him to choose a wife. They had this expectation with particular keenness before his grandfather started divesting himself of most of his wealth, but even without a large inheritance assured, Jesus was considered a solid match, though he showed no special favor to any woman, though he was kind to all. He had already made his peace with not ever having a wife or family and was anxious to get out into the world and begin to talk to more than just the children of Nazareth about what was important in life. Whenever he seemed especially restless I'd suggest another trip to the Sea of Galilee, and he always responded with a happy yes.

It was one full day's journey to get there. Our faithful donkey Sarah had finally passed on a few years before; the pack animal we took in his place was sufficient to our needs though he just did not have Sarah's almost loving personality. Over the years we had walked to many different spots on the lake, and we always did well with our fishing, so well that we often shared our catch with others who were having less luck. Of course, there were numerous commercial fishermen in those waters because the salting and pickling industry, based in the town of Magdala, exported the fish of that lake both far and near, even as far away as Rome. Jesus asked me to head for the waters near Magdala this time, as he was more and more anxious to see crowds of people. I knew he longed to talk to them, preach to them even, but he felt somehow, even as we his parents did, that his time had not yet come. There was still time, then, to enjoy a fishing trip for its own merits: relaxation, the excitement of not knowing what you might catch, the fight with the fish to land it, the reward of an excellent meal cooked over an open fire.

There were many boats of various sizes docked at Magdala and the early morning of our first day of fishing we saw most of them headed into the waters. I had over the years developed a better and better kind of fishing pole, and also made advances with both lines and hooks; being a skilled craftsman had its advantages. But an hour or so before noon we had caught a number of tilapia, which we caught on bread balls and a half dozen binny, which we caught readily on pieces of the sardines we purchased at a good price at the local fish market. These binny were much larger than the tilapia; even two of them would have been enough to feed us for the day. We also caught a catfish even larger than the binny, also on a bread ball, but of course we let it go, since it was not a fish we could eat.

We stopped fishing a little before noon, since the bites had slowed down and it was almost time for lunch. We decided to walk to the market and maybe trade some of our larger fish for more sardines for bait. A fish merchant readily accepted the deal and told us any time we wanted to trade biny for sardines he was the man to contact. We thanked him and continued to walk around the market place, since Jesus loved everything about it: the fish, the traders from foreign lands, the hustle of the whole environment, even the strong smell of fish. So it was that we happened upon a small group of fishermen who seemed to be in an altercation with a woman. When we got closer, though, we realized that the encounter was pretty one-sided, with the young woman clearly in command.

"You promised me a load of sardines and you didn't deliver. That's your problem not mine, am I right?"

"Of course, Mary, but…"one of the fishermen tried to interject, but the woman cut him off:

"But nothing, you dope. I don't need any buts, I need sardines. We can't sell your promises to the Romans. And I can't extend you a bit more credit. I'll take possession of your boat if I have to. You're the sorriest lot of fishermen I've ever had to deal with."

This woman amazed me and I could see she was having the same effect on Jesus. She was yelling at these men, five men in all, three of whom were particularly burly and tough looking characters, but it was they who were afraid of her. In spite of her loud voice and coarse language, she was a pretty, petite woman maybe only a year or three older than Jesus, with hair that was curly and reddish brown, a nose that was like an eagle's and hazel eyes lit up with energy and command. One of the men, perhaps the leader of their group, tried to appease her.

"Mary, you know we have always delivered the goods we promised. I mean, you can't blame us if the sardines haven't jumped in our boat. It's not as easy as you think. Some weeks the catch is not as certain as others. There's no reason for threats."

The woman shook her head and then stamped her foot before going back to yelling: "I'm not running a charity here, Simon. Bring me that huge load of sardines you promised or leave your fishing boat with me here and walk back to Capernaum. Maybe you'll have better luck at dusk. You'd better hope so."

With this the woman waved them away with a look of contempt in her eyes and went to talking to the next person waiting to address her. The men started to walk away, but Jesus decided to approach them.

"I've always wanted to go out on a boat in these waters," he told the man named Simon, a large, muscular man with a heavy, dark beard and the smell of the waters as his own kind of cologne.

"And why should I give a rat's rear about what you have always wanted, stranger?" Simon asked.

Jesus just smiled at him, not taking any offense, so the man called Simon continued: "Maybe you have something there, though, buddy," he smirked, with a look towards his companions. "We could just give up being fishermen and charter the boat to out-of-towners like this guy." The others laughed, a little rudely I thought, and then Simon continued, "Beat it, brother. We haven't got time for joking around. I'm about to lose my boat. Ever since that Mary's father croaked and left her to run the business she's been a she-devil to work with. What a drag that the guy didn't have any sons. We might as well take another shot at it, though, guys, whaddya say?"

"I say that I'd really like to join you on your boat if you have room. My father and I have pretty good luck finding fish; I think we'd do even better with a boat," Jesus said, still gently, still with a smile.

Simon turned back to Jesus and I was afraid he might get physical; he seemed the type who would be quick to anger. Another man, who resembled Simon, though not quite as foreboding, broke in, "Listen, friend, we really can't take on any amateurs. Go on your way and with the Lord's blessing."

"Thank you, friend," Jesus responded. "I'm trying to deliver that blessing to you and your shipmates now. We really are a pretty lucky pair. What have you to lose?"

Simon turned to the other man and laughed. "Sure, why not, Andrew? Bring the tourists along. Maybe they'll get sea sick and we can use their vomit for chum." The man called Simon then glared at Jesus: "Or maybe I'll throw you in the drink myself if you badger me anymore while on board. How about it, fellow? You really want on?"

I was about to step in but Jesus had remained calm the entire time and just nodded at the angry fisherman. "Thank you for the invitation. We accept. When are you going out next?"

"Not for hours," Andrew answered. "You can't catch sardines this time of day."

"If I were a betting man, I'd wager you could," Jesus responded. "We should go out right after lunch and I'm sure you'll do well."

"Now he's telling us when to go out," Simon laughed. "This fellow is either a prophet or a maniac. Hell, why not go out earlier? We should be out the whole time because if we don't have a load by sunset we're screwed. Which is it, brother, prophet or madman?" Simon asked, as he actually put his nose almost up against my son's.

"I'll let you decide that later," Jesus answered. "We're ready when you are."

When we did get on the boat there were several other men we hadn't met yet present; it was certainly the biggest boat we had ever been on, with a crew of close to a dozen men. We essentially replaced two of the original crew, hired men who had decided there would be no further payment forthcoming from Simon and his brother. I guessed this was at least partly why Simon had agreed to take us on. If they did happen upon a great load of sardines, they could use two more able bodied men to haul in the catch. Luckily, the fishermen's contempt for us began to temper a bit when they saw the fishing poles, lines and hooks I had fashioned myself, with Jesus's help.

"You say you made these things yourselves," another man, who identified himself as James, asked. "These are real beauties, and I've never seen a hook with a cleaner design," he added. "Look at this workmanship," he encouraged Simon.

"What good'll that do us?" he asked. "You can't catch sardines on a hook. Those sardines they're using for bait might be the only ones we'll see. But let's get out there and hope the Lord will sustain us."

Simon went to attend to the maneuvering of the boat. James said to us, in a far gentler tone than we had heard thus far. "He's not that bad a guy, really. It's just that he took the loan out to buy his own boat because he was tired of working for others, and he just got married and his mother-in-law doesn't think much of him, so he's dreading having to admit he failed. The poor dope is in over his head, you know."

"I know all about in-laws," I assured the man. "But I also know my son – don't lose hope."

After we were well into the waters of the lake, Jesus asked the men to steer the boat over to a spot a good distance from where Simon had first ordered the nets lowered and much closer to the shore. Simon objected, "Listen, pal, this time of day if by some miracle we'd run into a school of sardines, it would have to be in deep water. There's no way going your way is going to work. We can't afford to waste time."

"If by some miracle," Jesus repeated, with a look as well as tone of teasing affection towards the burly, unhappy man. I thought for certain I'd have to keep Simon from knocking Jesus into the lake, but somehow Jesus's total lack of fear of the bigger man and also something about his confidence goaded Simon to give the order to get to where Jesus had said to go.

"My son has always been a marvel at knowing where the fish are," I explained to Andrew, who was closest to me. "It's a real gift, that's the only way to explain it."

"We could use a gift, friend," he answered.

Why was it that I was certain we would find the fish we sought? I knew who Jesus was but the world did not and his heavenly father had shown no inclination to work miracles through his son. Yet he really always had had this particular special talent and I'd always felt it was somehow connected to bigger things to come.

So I was actually surprised when the first lowering of the nets at Jesus's behest resulted in an empty net. Simon was not surprised.

"Well, it's no harm done, since no one is going to catch sardines mid-afternoon, but maybe now we can at least ignore this nut and head for deeper waters, okay?"

"I only get one try?" Jesus asked. "I've always found magic in the number three. Won't you indulge me a bit longer?" he asked.

"So long as we are here near this shore, why not take another try or two?" James offered.

"Because it's crazy and a waste of time and effort? Is that a good enough reason?" Simon shouted.

Somehow James and Andrew had caught something from Jesus that gave them a bit of hope. They motioned me and other members of the crew to help them and without Simon's assistance cast the net another time, but it again landed them nothing. Simon laughed. "How many times do I have to deny this fool before you'll stop sweating for nothing?"

"If you deny me, you deny yourself, Simon," Jesus answered. "For these fish we'll bring up are for your sake, not mine. Let's try just a bit further south," Jesus suggested.

Simon seemed now almost to want Jesus to fail and was willing to let him have the opportunity. He even for the first time helped in the lowering of the net. It was James, though who first noticed, it was James who shouted when he realized their net was filling up, though it only took a moment more for his happy shock to spread when it was clear the net was filled so completely that it was threatening to be torn to pieces. It took the entire crew, using all our strength to get the net close to the surface and we had to signal another boat to help us, since there wasn't room enough for all those thousands of tiny fish on the boat. "You can have half the profit on any you carry for us," Simon promised and the strangers, with an empty boat to that point, readily agreed.

"How in the world did you do that?" James wondered as he slapped Jesus on the back.

"This saves the day, eh?" Andrew rejoiced.

"It saves the boat, that's for sure," Simon responded. "And listen, you, Jesus, is it? Anytime you want to shift careers and become a fisherman, you've got a job waiting for you. With your fish sense and my experience we'd be the top outfit on these waters. You were made for it, pal."

All of Simon's animosity and tension and anger were gone. I could tell he was the volatile type and that when he was happy, he'd be happy enough for five men and when he was your friend, he'd be the type who would die for you. I'll confess, though, I didn't really like the look in Jesus's eyes when he answered his sudden new friend.

"I might take you up on that someday, fisherman. I think fishing might just be something I'd really enjoy. I'd cast a wide net."

"Yeah, you're a natural, pal. I'll have to keep you away from that Mary of Magdala, though or she'll put you to work for her. You're going to be my little secret for now, okay?"

"For now, certainly," Jesus answered. "My time has not yet come."

Chapter Twenty-Three

It was about a year after that fishing trip that the old nightmares returned, along with some new ones that were just as disturbing. Jesus was a grown-up now, but his nightmares were so intense and his cries in the night so poignant, that it felt like he was just a little boy and we were failing to relieve him of his fears. No matter how much his mother and I had been warned about the suffering to come, I refused to believe it could be as bad as the nightmares predicted. I insisted, again and again, that it was the devil's work, his attempt to undo our faith. "If we've found the devil, father, then where are the angels?" Jesus would ask me. And I didn't have an answer. I prayed for one, as did his mother, even more incessantly than I, but almost every night we'd be awakened by our son's cries.

Jesus could not bear to relate the content of the new nightmares with his mother present, but at times in the workshop he would share them with me. "Time and again now I dream of men, men in black robes, who speak my name and claim a special privilege from knowing me well. They seem wise like our priests and also kind and caring for all. But then the dreams shift to some of them taking in children with their 'kindness' and then doing horrible things to those children, things they insist the children never speak of. And the dream lets me see the horrible pain the children are left to suffer, and the respect and authority the men who have betrayed them continue to have. It makes me crazy to even think of someone harming a child in any way, so the idea that a person could say he is a special follower of mine but then would so harm a child, even as a dream it tortures me beyond reason, makes me want to do physical harm to these men, so that they might never harm another child."

Jesus told me all this in a fairly calm voice until the last few lines. By his story's end he was more tense and disturbed than I had ever seen him when fully awake. I didn't know how to respond. I kept to my usual strategy, even though I was myself beginning to doubt my own words.

"Again I ask you, my son, why would the Most High allow such cruelty? And how could anyone who claims connection to you, which is connection and identity with the Most High, how could a person ever act as in your dreams? His place in

Hell would be secured. But even beyond that, how could any man be so evil? These are just the devil's ways to test you. You have to try to stay strong."

Jesus appreciated my efforts and just the opportunity to tell me his woe, but I could see he was as confused as ever about the torture of his nightmares. Neither of us understood why his heavenly father was not giving him some positive sign, some affirmation of his role as Messiah to his people, rather than letting the devil inflict him with horror and doubt with all these visions of an evil future that was somehow Jesus's own fault. All Jesus did each day was work hard for me in the shop, help his mother with chores, go out and feed the poor and the sick, visit with the lepers who no one else would go near, make toys for the little children and tell them stories, study the sacred books and discuss them with the elders, and pray each day many times more than required of even the most observant Jew. In all things Jesus remained as patient and kind and loving as his mother herself had always been. And for this he was made to suffer, with the devil constantly by his side each night, but no help from any heavenly beings.

Mary and I grew ever closer with this common ground of pity and worry over Jesus. Her beautiful eyes, which had not dimmed with age, were often glistening with tears and her prayers too were perpetual. Unlike Jesus and me, though, she had confidence, unwavering confidence in our Lord. "Give yourself to the Most High and know he is watching over you, my son," she would say. "The Lord loves all his creatures, the birds and bugs and flowers, even the weeds, are always provided for. Surely, his own beloved Son he will watch over and lead to triumph and glory."

I never had the heart to respond to her, "The birds eat the bugs and are themselves savaged and eaten by bigger birds. The fawn is not moments from its mother's womb before it is taken by the jackal, torn to pieces and devoured. Does this too come from your all-loving Lord?" These thoughts I kept to myself, while continuing to pray that the boy I had seen grow into such a good man would not be torn apart by his heavenly father's inscrutable will, the same will that had made me sacrifice an ordinary married life for a secret celibacy that now seemed to make less sense than ever, since all I had tried to do for his Son was not seeming to have mattered much at all.

Things got still worse. The next set of nightmares was about, of all things, wood. Jesus woke up a few hours after midnight screaming, "No, take that cross away from me, no, no don't make me carry it, no!" After lighting a lantern I raced into his room because he seemed to be thrashing around enough to hurt himself. Mary followed right behind. "The Romans. The Romans were forcing me to carry one of their crosses, the ones they use to crucify criminals. 'I'm not a criminal' I kept telling them, but they wouldn't listen. They insisted I carry the cross. They lashed me again and again until I took it up again. I repeated, 'I am no criminal. I want to fill the world with love,' but they only laughed and lashed my back all the more."

"You will never be a criminal; the Romans will never have cause or chance to harm you, my son," Mary said and I wanted to believe her and so I said, "Of course, that's right." But neither Jesus nor I really believed what Mary was saying. We knew dreams meant something and what good thing could come from nightmares like these? Mary still sought to console her son. She sat down at his bedside and she tried to give him a hug. But under his thin sleep garment Mary could easily feel his flesh. And when she embraced him, she soon shuddered with surprise.

"Oh, my poor son, what is wrong with your back?"

A tilt of the lantern and I could see that the garment was streaked with red. Jesus, the son of the Most High, had lacerations across his back, like those caused by a vicious scourging, though there was no whip anywhere to be found, nowhere, at least, in our waking world, but the blood was certainly real.

The physical wounds healed, healed more quickly than I had imagined they would, but the mental damage remained. Jesus could no longer work with wood; he shuddered even at the sight of the wood in our workshop. He tried valiantly to get over his fear, but he just couldn't stay in our shop without breaking down. I told him we could take a vacation, spend some time with Simon and Andrew, James and the others we had seen a few times more over the past year. "I don't think a vacation will help me. I'll pray for some relief from a surer source." So I went back to working by myself, hoping he was wrong, hoping he would soon be able to return, if only to continue to make toys for the little children who loved his handicraft so well. Even the children, though, reminded him of his nightmares. He was lost in his own home, his own town. And I had nothing to give him that might help.

We weren't very surprised then when one night at supper he announced that he was leaving.

"I'm going to go take Simon up on his offer and become a fisherman. Maybe I can find some relief there, some calming from the Sea of Galilee."

"But the boats are made of wood," I reminded him. "And the life of a fisherman is no life for a reverent man, especially one who is also so skilled in craft."

"Even a fisherman can be holy," Jesus responded, "as a priest may be wicked," and he looked at me with all the sorrow of the past months drawn deep into his blue grey eyes. "Perhaps in Magdala or Capernaum I can find peace or at least discover something more than what I've known here."

"Will you abandon your parents as they grow older?" Mary asked him. "If your time has come to serve your people Israel, that is one thing, but to go fishing for a life, is that really what the Most High decrees?"

Mary had that tone she almost always maintained, a beat short of smug in her confidence of what would be the right thing in any situation. But Jesus was now an adult and not bound to agree with everything his mother believed.

"When my heavenly father wants me to serve him, he will let me know. Meanwhile, I will serve him and honor my earthly parents by maintaining my virtue and my love of neighbor wherever I should go."

The next day he left, with some supplies, including a few of my fishing poles, though I knew he was destined mostly for work with a net from now on. He didn't promise even to return for visits, but I encouraged him not to forget how much his mother would miss him.

"And you, father, will you also miss me?"

"If what you're doing will relieve your pain or help you in any way, I'll be glad that you're gone. Plus, I still love to fish; you won't mind if I visit you, do you?"

"I will always be your son, my father, and always filled with joy at the sight of you."

With that he embraced me and soon he was on his way. I felt a sort of peace in that embrace, a feeling that maybe this leave taking was the start of some sort of understanding to come, though I had no clue as to why I felt that way.

Chapter Twenty-Four

The first time I visited Jesus he was living in Capernaum, actually staying with the fisherman Simon and his extended family, including a wife, a mother-in-law, a widowed sister of his mother-in-law, her teenaged son and Simon's own brother Andrew. There wasn't room for me, but I had brought our tent so I was not concerned; really, I was happy to have an excuse not to have to reside, even for a day or two, in such a noisy, crowded household. Shouting seemed their preferred way of communication and usually it wasn't because anyone was angry but rather that they seemed to like to make everything they said seem important by supporting it with a loud emphasis. Simon's mother-in-law was especially loud and never worried once about hurting anyone's feelings. "Why can't you be more like your friend Jesus?" she would ask Simon. "He's every bit the fisherman you are, but so polite and he washes up before he comes inside smelling like a sardine. You should be proud of him, Joseph. Oh, and you taught him well – he's already fixed two or three things around the house I've been asking my lazy son-in-law to fix for months. What a good son, you have, and a skilled craftsman."

Apparently Jesus had gotten over his fear of wood, or his politeness and willingness to help others had helped him overcome his reluctance to work again as a craftsman. Overall, Jesus seemed a lot more relaxed. He kept laughing at the various yarns the fishermen wove, both in the boat and at the supper table, he kept finding Simon's family charming, no matter how loud they became, though he himself had lived under the always calm auspices of his mother. To speak truly, though Simon's mother-in-law seemed at first like a shrew, once you spent more than a few minutes with her you realized it was her way and that she really didn't always mean any harm, nor even dislike her son-in-law. On the contrary, with the success that Jesus's joining the boat crew had gained for him, Simon was now in his family's best graces, his wife and in-laws happy to enjoy the benefits of all the new prosperity. "I tell you, Joseph, since your son joined us we're breaking records, if records of such things were ever kept. That fishmonger Mary is in shock with how much we bring her. I've got my boat paid off in full now, so I'm out of her clutches. I've got to keep my eye on her, though. She spends too much time pestering Jesus. I'm afraid she's going to make him a better offer, one that will be hard to refuse, if you know what I mean."

With this line, Simon winked at me, one man-of-the-world to another. If he only knew how unlike the usual men of our time I and Jesus were, he would have done something besides wink, I'm certain. What struck me most about Simon, though, and to a lesser extent his brother and the other fishermen was that they had a genuine affection now for Jesus. And it wasn't just about how good he was at finding fish for them. They listened with attention if at times bemusement to all he had to say about taking care of the poor or being kind to strangers; this message fell pretty naturally on their ears, as in their prosperity they did not begrudge the amounts Jesus asked them to hand over to the less fortunate. In fact, when I saw them sharing not only some of their catch but at times the profits from that catch with strangers, they seemed actually to enjoy it and Jesus could see that and it made him very glad. Back in Nazareth people had always questioned his generosity, as if he were trying to make himself seem better than them, but here on the Sea of Galilee they just thought Jesus was a good mate, someone who wanted everyone to have enough to eat, and they saw nothing at all wrong with that.

The one exception within his new group of friends and associates was Mary of Magdala. Maybe it was because she was in charge of a large commercial fish salting and pickling business and as a woman felt she had to be all the more hard-edged and shrewd to not be taken advantage of or underestimated by all the men who she had to continue to impress. Maybe it was just her nature, which seemed unnatural for a woman just because one did not encounter many women in charge of a business at all, much less a big and thriving one. Simon was right, she was very interested in Jesus, but when we encountered her while unloading some fish in Magdala, I could tell her feelings for my son were about as complicated as she herself was.

"Why do you stay with these louts?" she questioned my son as we were transferring the catch. "I can tell just by looking at you that you're a man of some culture, unlike your hairy friends."

"My friends suit me well; I look for none better," Jesus answered her with a smile. "By the way, this is my father, Joseph the Craftsman. Perhaps you have heard of the quality of his work even here in Magdala."

"Yes, I have. I hope he hasn't lost his mind too and decided to forego the hammer and saw for fishing nets."

"I'm just a visitor here," I told her. "I've come to see my son. His friends have been most gracious to me," I added, feeling somehow a need to defend Simon and his crew.

"Nothing you say in our defense will impress this slave driver," Simon laughed. "But I appreciate the try."

We had gotten most of the fish off the boat by this time. Mary turned to me and surprised me by actually grabbing me by the arm as she said: "Joseph, perhaps you can advise your son better than these fools. If he comes to work for me, he'd soon be second in command and making more profit in a month than these characters could make in years, especially once they'd lost his magic touch."

"I think my son is happy as he is. He's never cared about wealth."

"But I know he cares about the poor," she continued, still holding onto my arm, in a way that was some odd combination of insistence and flirtation: "Isn't the best way to help them to have as much wealth as possible to share?"

"Woman, with all your wealth, where is your portion for your neighbors?" Jesus asked, not with harsh judgment, but still some challenge in his voice

"Am I responsible for all the foolish men who are too lazy to work? No one need starve with so many fish in the sea."

"There are widows, orphans, the elderly. Do you have fish for them?" he asked.

Simon, Andrew and the others began to pay attention to this give and take. It seemed they were happy to find a man who could go back and forth with this woman who had them all cowed.

"I have work even for them. I am a woman without a husband and, see, I do not starve," she said, as she gestured to all the fish in her hold.

"No, you will never lack for things to feed your body," Jesus nodded.

"Again, I ask you, Jesus, why not work for me and then with your profits you can share all you want with the poor. Meanwhile let me store my treasure as I see fit."

Jesus sat down on the dock and invited Mary to sit beside him. She surprised all the men by taking him up on the offer. "Mary, I heard once of a man who had great wealth. One year his harvest was so great he didn't have room to store all of his bounty. So he said to himself, 'I'm going to tear down my old barns and build larger ones to store all my goods. Then I will for years ahead just eat, drink and make merry.' But that same man did not last through the night. What do you think the Lord said to him when he had passed from this earth?"

"I won't presume to know what the Most High might say or think," Mary answered almost coyly.

"Pardon my pride, then if I do feel comfortable so to presume, if only for the sake of my story. For surely, you'd agree, the Lord must say, 'The things you have stored and prepared, to whom will they belong?' Thus will it be for all who store up treasure for themselves but are not rich in what matters to the Most High."

"You do presume, fisherman," Mary concluded, as she raised herself up from her seat on the dock. Jesus too got up and added: "Woman, never deny your true nature. Your happiness will only come when you are such as these men, who love life but do not ignore those with less fortune than they."

"Perhaps I need guidance, rabbi," she responded, again with a sharp coyness that she wore well with her blazing eyes and hair the color of sunset.

"I am no teacher, Mary of Magdala. Not yet. Now still is the time to learn."

"I would be happy to teach you, then, my Jesus. I still think you'd learn more from me than your present companions."

With those words she walked dismissively away, but then turned back to us, shouting, "And get that ugly boat launched and out of my dock. I have many more to do business with today."

"You really gave her the business, eh Nazarene?" Simon laughed. "That was worth the trip even if we had come over without a single sardine."

"She's an interesting woman. I think she might someday do wonderful things," Jesus said.

"She's a wonder all right," Simon laughed before slapping Jesus on the back and then re-boarding the boat to get away from both Magdala and Mary.

I stayed a few days longer than I had originally intended; I hadn't given my own Mary an exact date when I expected to return, so I hoped she wouldn't worry. I was just pretty taken by how Jesus was changing, growing more confident in his ideas and finding comfort in living this life with these men and women. I realized that I was actually having fun, laughing and smiling more than I had since, well, since ever. These fishermen respected Jesus but didn't take him too seriously, and Jesus seemed to like that mix well. There was no talk of nightmares or future destiny. He was living life day to day and enjoying every moment, every conversation, every scene. I didn't know whether his mother would approve; I didn't know how long it could last, but for a few days at least, I didn't care.

Two days later, on the boat ride back to Capernaum, after having left yet another good catch at Magdala, with no tasks beyond keeping the boat afloat, we all had more time to talk and these men loved to talk. Even more they loved to argue and a conversation between Andrew and his brother Simon soon got so heated that Simon offered to "make your fat nose even fatter," to which Andrew replied, "No matter how I'd bash that head of yours, I doubt I could make it any fatter, but I don't mind trying if you're man enough to do more than bluster." Young John, the brother of James, who had only recently been added to the crew, stepped in between the two brothers, and tried to stop their fighting, with soothing words and a plea for reason. He was less strong than either of the brothers and was not going to be able to keep them apart for long. Simon yelled at James, "Get your little brother out of the way; I have no quarrel with him, though nobody likes a meddler. Tell him to mind his own business."

Jesus now stepped in between the two men as well, in fact grabbed Simon by his right arm so he could not launch his stronger fist at either John or Andrew. He said to Simon, "What you say isn't true. I say blessed are the peace makers, for to me they are the real children of the Lord."

"Who asked you?" Simon shot back, though with some embarrassment, once he realized that Jesus had gripped him in such a way that he was fairly helpless to resist. "Andrew and I argue all the time; it never comes to anything. You both should mind your own business."

"The boy was doing the right thing. Admit that and I'll let off my grip on you."

"I'll admit no such thing," Simon remained stubborn. "I say rather, 'Woe to him who puts his nose where it doesn't belong, for he shall see stars,' if you know what I mean."

Here John's brother James piped in, "You don't seem capable of delivering much woe at the moment, plus if you lay a hand on my little brother, you're the one who will be seeing stars."

Somehow James's tone belied any real threat, such that Simon was able to laugh and say to Jesus, "Fine, the peace makers are the Lord's children. I can't afford to fight with you anyway, or I lose my meal ticket, right? Another year or two with you and we'll all be rich, right?"

Jesus let Simon go with a gentle pat on the shoulder. He then said, "Simon, were you not listening when I spoke with Mary. I say also, 'Woe to those who are rich, for they are receiving their comfort now.'"

"What's wrong with a little comfort?" Andrew asked, ready now to take his brother's side. "Is it better to be miserable? To be poor and hungry?"

The boat started to rock a little and I could see that the wind had suddenly picked up and there were now clouds where there hadn't been any just a few moments before. Still the men kept minimal attention on the boat's direction, while they continued to argue.

"There are worse things than being physically poor. And those who hunger for more than food and drink, but rather for what is right, they too are blessed, for theirs is a hunger that will be satisfied," Jesus insisted.

"You seem to have been giving this a lot of thought," Simon said in a more serious tone. "You really think it's better to be poor than rich, better to be lowly than exalted? What have you been teaching this son of yours, Joseph? I thought two working men like yourselves would have learned that life isn't all what the holy books tell us it is."

"His mother and I taught him to love the Lord more than anything and to love his neighbor as himself and he has always followed that advice, which comes straight from the Most High," was my simple response.

"But who is my neighbor?" James wanted to know. "Surely you two don't think we should love that skinflint Mary, or tax collectors or other thieves, not to mention the Samaritans or the Lord forbid, Romans?"

Jesus turned towards James, shook his head, but then spoke: "I've been think-ing about this a lot. What merit comes to a man who is good to his children and close friends only? Thieves and Romans do the same, no? What good is it to lend money only to those we are certain will pay it back? I think we need to do good even to those who hate us, I think we should give to anyone who asks something of us and expect no return, I think we need to love everyone, not just those who love us already. That's what I've come to believe. Blessed are those who are merci-ful, who do not judge, who care for others with no expectation of reward. Their reward will last forever."

This time Simon laughed aloud. "I didn't know you were such a dreamer. But, hey, I can agree with some of what you say. I'm ready to love any woman, given she's no dog, whether she loves me or not. Just don't tell my wife, okay?"

The men laughed, except for young John, who seemed to be very taken with all that Jesus was saying. Jesus frowned at Simon's joke and his whole attitude and said to him a little sharply. "My father does not favor that kind of humor."

Simon was taken aback, looked at me, an older man, with some chagrin and apologized, "Sorry, Joseph, it's all in good fun, you know."

"I don't think Jesus was talking about me," I answered him.

"Who then?" he asked, genuinely confused.

"Hey, you guys, forget that for now – look ahead," Andrew cautioned.

Seemingly out of nowhere some scary dark clouds had appeared and were mov-ing towards us rapidly. The wind picked up quickly and violently and almost be-fore the men could prepare for it, heavy rain assailed us. Storms were not every day occurrences, but also not totally unusual, but we soon discovered that these par-ticular clouds had seemed to settle just over our boat without much coverage of the water in any direction. But as we tried to proceed towards shore, the clouds seemed to follow us and continued to buffet us and render our one sail useless. The hired men who made up the additional work force looked particularly afraid, though all of us but one were of course frightened. That one was Jesus, who seemed to enjoy the rain, and said to Simon, "I told you he wouldn't like that joke of yours."

"Oh, that father," Simon shouted over the storm. "Well, hey, I'm sorry, then, but a fat lot of good that will do us now. Help with the bailing, will you? Or are you only good for finding fish? Soon we'll be swimming with them if you don't help."

Instead of grabbing a bucket, Jesus raised his hands to the sky. His lips began to move, but we could not hear what he was saying. But only a moment or two after he started, the clouds broke up, the wind died down and then disappeared and the sun reigned so fully that the only evidence of a storm was how wet we all still were. The men looked on with amazement at Jesus, who calmly but firmly shook his head like a dog who shakes the water off his coat. A few of the crew were still frightened, one of them whispering to his companion, "Wizard, magician."

"No such thing," Jesus laughed. "Those storms come and go in a minute this time of year. You know that Simon, don't you?"

Simon was silent for a moment but then replied, "Certainly, I've seen some fast passing storms on these waters, but it seemed like you called up to Heaven and then the storm was gone, as if at your command."

"No, I just made a simple prayer to the father, like any one of you could have done."

"He's Neptune himself, I tell you," I heard one of the hired men mutter to his companion. "He rules the fish and commands the storms to come and go."

Jesus, overhearing the man, responded, "Please don't bring up the names of false gods. There is but one Lord, the father of us all, and whatever you ask of him, you will receive. You might all do better to pray more to the father."

Simon shook his head. "Are you a prophet then, Jesus of Nazareth? Why have you come among us then, poor fishermen who know no better?"

"No, I am no prophet, Simon. And there has been no magic here. Who knows what the future holds for us, but I tell you when I am ready, I will look to exalt the poor and the powerless and I know the Lord will reward the kind hearted, the generous, the downtrodden, those who can keep their faith no matter what storm assails them. I believe you can be such a man, friend Simon. But my time has not yet come."

We reached Capernaum without further incident. The men all had been put in a somber and uncharacteristically silent mood. I said to Jesus when we were a bit apart from the others, "Perhaps your time draws near."

Chapter Twenty-Five

In spite of my prediction and my hope, Jesus's time did not come soon and his mother and I remained without him in Nazareth for more than another year. During that time Mary suffered greatly. When Jesus was young and mostly a happy child Mary's life had been happy, confident as she was that we were honored and blessed to be the parents of the Messiah and that he would restore Israel to its proper place for the nation of God's chosen people. As Jesus grew older and seemed not to be finding his place in the world, her confidence wavered, not in the Lord's might and Jesus's destiny, but rather in what form that destiny would take and how it could lead to glory. And then Jesus left and her whole purpose in life was in question. And then things got worse still when within two months of each other, her one close friend, our Bethlehem benefactress, Ruth and her beloved father Joachim both died.

As nice a person as Mary always was, she didn't make friends easily. Most of the women assumed since she had come from wealth and had always been so reverent and prayerful and more learned than a woman was expected to be that she would think others inferior. For this reason, her kindness to the poor, her gentle ways, her refusal to partake in gossip, were all more signs to those women that she thought herself superior to them. Only Ruth, who we often tried to see during our fairly frequent visits to Jerusalem, was somehow able to see the real Mary, how genuine and kind and unassuming she really was. Ruth, childless herself, always loved seeing Jesus, whom she treated like a favorite nephew. When she passed away suddenly from a fever, her husband Micah hadn't time to send word before we instead heard it from him directly when we stopped in Bethlehem. I tried to console Micah as well as I could, but all his success as an innkeeper and landlord now meant nothing to him without his life partner. Mary herself had trouble consoling him because she was so in need of consolation herself. She mourned Ruth's death for many weeks, weeks when her eyes looked less hopeful than I had ever seen them look. And just when she was maybe close to recovering, word came that her father needed us at his house immediately, for he had suffered great pain in his heart.

Joachim's transformation had continued over the past few years to the point that many of the possessions that had adorned his home were no longer there, as he had either given away or sold them to continue to share what he had with the less fortunate. He had become beloved by the poor but considered crazy by people of his own social class. When we went to his bedside, I could tell he was holding on just so he could say goodbye.

"Mary, my jewel, my blessing from above, I thank the Most High that he gave me a long enough life to mend my ways and to try to do right by all his children. After so many years of the gift of your grace and love, I would have been damned to have learned nothing from your example. And your son, through him you reached me and brought me now to a place of peace."

"Father, your blessings have been with me always. Through your kindness and love for me, you practiced the way of loving all your neighbors."

"Too long practicing, too little doing, but at least I've had these past few years, my child," Joachim responded with a weak smile.

I didn't think Joachim would have anything in particular to say to me; even after his transformation he and I had not become that much closer, but I was wrong. "Joseph, my son, you must forgive an old man before he departs this world," he said as he actually reached for my hand.

"I have nothing to forgive," I told him, but he squeezed my hand, with surprising strength and looked me directly in the eye.

"Let us have some honesty now. If not now, when? Because I cherished my daughter so completely and because she was so exceptional, no man would ever have satisfied me. But you have been always patient, respectful and always a good provider and a wonderful father to my grandson. No man, really, could ever have been better. I give you my blessing as I depart, and ask you to forgive my years of unkindness."

"My father, your daughter is a jewel, a treasure, so how can I blame you for your reluctance to see her married to a simple craftsman? But if you insist, yes, I'll forgive you, even as I ask the Lord above to forgive my own unworthiness"

These words seemed to please him. He did not let go of his grip on my hand, though, but rather signaled Mary to take hold of the other. We recited prayers together as we ushered him on to the next life. He died a comforted man, who had done much to merit the love of all.

Whatever was left of his estate went of course to me and Mary. He had specified that we were to continue to share with the poor, though he knew we would have done so without his prompting. Mary and I had each passing year less need of material things. She was a fine cook but our fare was simple; she kept our home clean and our clothing mended and we kept a fire for when we needed one, and nothing else was required by way of physical comfort. But Mary needed something after these losses and I struggled to find a way to help her through her pain.

When Jesus lived with us it was easier to find release in my work with him, in the conversations he and I would have or those we three would have together, in the laughter we would sometimes share, in the fishing trips or building of toys for the children or our visits with those children and their families. Mary and I continued those visits, but without Jesus there, with his storytelling and loving presence, it wasn't quite the same. And once Joachim died, Mary needed a rest from those visits and just went about her daily routine without a lot of joyfulness, though she continued to pray and to believe. I wanted to comfort her, but what does a person normally do when his beloved spouse is suffering? A good man, rather than complaining, would offer her an embrace, would take on some of her tasks, would talk to her with kindness. The latter two things I did without hesitation, but embraces were still off limits. I thought once I passed my fiftieth birthday that my longings might abate or even cease, but they had not. Mary was now somewhat frail and her hair had lots of grey, but she had only grown more beautiful to me. I prayed for guidance and for strength because I felt she needed me now more than ever with her son no longer with us. I had done a good job of not straying, of suffering my secret celibacy though I never really understood why it had to be this way, but now it wasn't my needs that mattered; I wanted to embrace my wife because I loved her and she needed an embrace.

We had just finished dinner three weeks to the day since Joachim had passed away. I was helping Mary to clean up and to store the leftover food. I noticed when I happened to look at her that tears were glistening her eyes.

"Mary, why are you crying? You know your father was blessed by the Lord; I know your faith consoles you, so why are you crying?"

"Oh, Joseph, your kindness, it's your kindness that fills my eyes with tears."

As a younger man I might have dismissed those words as the foolish thoughts of a woman, but I felt as if I understood what she meant and soon I myself was close to tears.

"You deserve every kindness, my bride, and I pray each night for forgiveness for the years I was less kind."

"Joseph," Mary said my name with such tenderness that my tears now could not be held back. "I have put you through so much, but it was all God's will, yet now I don't know what the Lord wants from us. Is our mission done, or have we failed our son who may be wasting his time as a fisherman when he was supposed to be the savior of our people? How can he be a savior when he spends his time with fishermen? I don't understand; I don't want to have put you through this lonely life all for nothing. Can you forgive me? Can you, Joseph, my love?"

Her blue-grey eyes were still as large, as beautiful and as much the light from a holy woman's soul as ever. I could not spend another second thinking or worrying about what I should do. I took my wife in a strong embrace, I pushed her greying hair back from her tearful eyes. I kissed her gently on the cheek and told her: "There is nothing to forgive, Mary, my bride. Who can deny the Lord's command? I know this all has been ordained. I know we have done the best we could. You have remained without sin and I have tried to become a better man through your example. Our son is destined for greatness, but maybe of a kind we never imagined. The Most High is beyond all understanding, but my love for you I now understand completely."

There wasn't a bit of lust or temptation in the embrace we shared. My care for poor Mary was what engulfed me, only what I could do to make her suffer less concerned me. Feeling this, knowing this, she did not try to get me to release her. We soon sat down again, next to each other, holding hands and I thanked the Lord for this small miracle, this gift I had waited so long to enjoy.

"Maybe there is something we can do," Mary decided. "Soon the Passover season will be upon us. Don't you think you could talk Jesus into traveling to the temple with us, as a family again? Do you think it might be possible? I need to know he is on the path ordained for him. Maybe he still needs our help to find it."

"Maybe he does. I'll go to Capernaum and talk with him. I'll try my best to bring him home to you."

A few days later I left, praying all the way that my perfect son would come back, for a little while at least, to bring some peace to my perfect wife.

Chapter Twenty-Six

I found Jesus in a state of crisis. The nightmares had returned, his ability to predict where the fish could be caught had left him and none of his fishermen friends seemed able to console him. They told me he was more and more reflective on the holy books, but that he had probably spent far more time than was healthy reading from the saddest of David's Psalms and the woeful words of the writer of Ecclesiastes. At close to thirty years of age, Jesus seemed like a man who thought his whole life to this point had been in vain, yet he had no clue what he should do next. My suggestion that he come home to see his mother and then journey with us to Jerusalem he did not take as providential, but since the joy and growth he had found in Capernaum seemed at an end, he agreed mostly for my sake and his mother's.

Jesus was tanned and lithe and lean. His beard and hair had been somewhat reddened by all his time in the sun and his hands were calloused from working the nets. He stood erect and thereby now was an inch or two taller than I, who had lost my best bearing from so many years stooped over a work bench or lathe. In spite of his good looks, his flowing hair, full beard and piercing blue-grey eyes, there was only sadness evident in his visage, a sadness I could not seem to shake him from as we wended our way back to Nazareth.

"The nightmares I find more and more convincing," he explained to me as we walked towards home with just our pack animal, a particularly high-strung mule, as our companion. "I see again and again the faces of all those who will suffer at the hands of people who claim to be my followers."

"But these are just the devil's games," I one more time insisted. "You are being tested, but you're too aware of God's love and mercy to believe this false future."

"I get no word from above. No angel has visited me as you say helped guide both you and my mother. I get only visions of torture and greed, of evil men claiming to be my disciples. And I myself see nothing but my own suffering ahead – visions of being beaten and made to carry a criminal's cross; these dreams too will not desert me."

I had no answers for him. I wanted so to believe that the life I had led must have had some purpose, some part in a final plan that was for the benefit of our people. But if this son of man who I also knew was the son of the Most High himself, if he was losing hope, what could I bring to him that he might believe?

Mary cried when she saw her son, cried and hugged and bestowed blessings upon him. Jesus himself broke down, apologizing to his mother for his long absence and asking her to forgive him.

"You who are incapable of any wrongdoing don't need to apologize to me. If I were stronger I would understand why you have done as you have done. I'm only glad to spend this time with you now. Will you go with us too to the temple for Passover?"

Jesus let her know he did plan to make the trip and we could see immediately how she brightened to know he would be with us, as in the old days, making the trip to not only the temple but also to Ain Karin to visit with Mary's amazing cousin Elizabeth.

Elizabeth was about eighty years old but still as vibrant and busy and kind as she had always been. Her son John also had not changed; he was as wild and impulsive and as given to bursts of enthusiasm as ever. Though some months older than Jesus he had never once in his life held down a steady job. From the priestly caste through his father, he had rejected that sacred profession, his mother having told us more than once that, "John just doesn't care for all the rules and rituals." When he wanted to help earn some money for the household, he hired out as a day laborer; his strength and physical abilities were unquestioned, so he never lacked for that sort of work when he sought it out, particularly since they lived so near the bustling Jerusalem. He preferred not to work at all, but instead went many times into the desert to pray and meditate; during those times, his mother told us, he subsisted on insects and wild honey, when he ate at all. He was a kind of mystic, though extremely outgoing when he wanted to be. I didn't mind his life choices except for the fact that his mother was old and her only son instead of caring for her in that old age, let her go on supporting herself. Elizabeth didn't seem to mind, though; she had started an informal kind of bakery years before, to share her honey cake and breads and other delicious confections with those who were less skilled in that art. She always had more orders than she could easily fill and still somehow had the energy and spirit to keep filling them. With my own son, like John unmarried and having spent the last few years of his life as a fisherman, I knew I was in no real position to judge.

Of course, I still wasn't prepared for this version of John we met up with when we reached Elizabeth's home. John opened the door for us and I thought I was looking at a madman. His hair was almost bleached by all his time in the hot sun; his eyes had a fire that seemed wild, and, like any wild fire potentially destructive. He bowed to Mary, gave me an embrace that shook my bones but then stepped back from Jesus and simply said, "Behold the Lamb of God, behold him who will take away the sins of this world." Jesus at first could not help but be taken aback, but then he smiled and said simply, "Yes, hello to you too, Cousin John."

One always ate well at Elizabeth's table and John was not in fasting mode for our first meal together; in fact he ate as if it were his last meal. Luckily, there was still more than enough for us all. After dinner, as we enjoyed a bit of a sweet wine that Elizabeth had concocted herself from wild berries John had gathered, John and Jesus suddenly got into a pretty heated discussion, at least on John's end of it.

"But I've been waiting now for years, for word of your ministry's beginning. And yet your parents tell us you've been off fishing. Nothing wrong with that, but enough is enough, right? When are you going to get going, cousin?"

"I don't know what you mean," Jesus replied calmly before sipping his wine and nodding to Elizabeth to show his approval.

"I know you're incapable of telling a lie, so when you say you don't know what I mean, that must be irony or some sort of joke, right? Of course you know exactly what I mean, lamb of God, so we can leave off all the joking for now, right?"

"I wish you wouldn't call me that. I'm no lamb, you know," Jesus said, still trying to sound and remain calm.

"The time for your preferences are past, son of man. It's time to fulfill your destiny. I'm practically bursting, holding back, waiting to prepare the way for you. There's only so much fasting a person can do."

"I don't understand, cousin. What do my future actions have to do with yours? How are you not free to do as you please?"

John got up from his chair and seemed to glare at Jesus. "If I didn't know better, I'd expect you to quote Cain next, 'Am I my brother's keeper?' You know very well why I'm waiting. From the time I leapt in my mother's womb upon your first entrance into this house, a story my mother has told me more than twice, you can imagine, you and I have been aligned. There's no use pretending to deny it; it comes too close to a sin for you to keep up this nonsense, cousin. You are the Christ, the anointed one; it's time to begin."

"Madman, what do you know of my beginnings? If you only knew my struggles. But I don't want to waste any more time discussing my duties with you."

Jesus fled from the room and soon outside the home. Mary looked at me, asked me to go and talk to him, but John said in a much calmer tone than I expected from him, "Leave him be for now. But soon we'll have to continue this discussion. Is there any more honey cake, mother?"

After an hour had passed I started to worry and went out looking for my son. I didn't really want John to come with me, but he insisted. Our main meal had been in mid-afternoon so it wasn't dark yet, but we brought lanterns along in case our search lasted for hours. Along the way I tried to convince John not to keep being so judging of Jesus.

"I'm in no position to judge, Cousin Joseph. Surely you understand none of us are in that position. But if he needs someone to goad him into action, I'm not afraid of being that guy. I fear nothing that can happen to me on this earth."

"And how did you come to be so brave?" I asked him.

"Oh, I'm not trying to brag. I just know what's ahead and so I'm not expecting anything but pain and suffering from this life."

"How is it you know all this? Are you a prophet then?"

"You, too, Joseph?" John asked, now exasperated with me as well. "It's like your whole family is trying to forget you've been visited by angels and destined for great things. Yes, Cousin Joseph, I am a prophet, and not just a prophet, *the last* prophet, the one who prepares the way of the Lord."

I grabbed this wild man by the arm, looked into his crazy eyes and asked: "How are you so certain of this? Have you had a sign? We've been waiting for one for years, but nothing has come, only nightmares. And I haven't seen an angel since Jesus was a small child. Only nightmares and not-knowing have besieged us."

"The time for visitations is nearly done. People will have to have faith without outward signs. And who should need a further sign than what can be read in the happy gurgle of a baby or even the howl of the wolf? God is everywhere, not just or especially in the temple. Man has squandered, again and again, his relationship with the Most High. But man's redeemer has come. I am his prophet. He is your son. Let's find him."

We discovered Jesus not five minutes later, sitting by himself just a short ways off from what passed for a road out of Ain Karin, as if he wanted us to find him or at least not go to too much trouble in our search.

"Father, I could not escape our cousin even if I tried, so I didn't bother. But, John, you don't do me justice entirely. It's not that I don't want to act. I just have worries that my actions will do more harm than good. I've had nightmare after nightmare. In them our own people, the people of Israel suffer greatly because of men and women who claim me as their own. And men of many nations kill and are killed in my name. My father tells me these are just attacks from the devil but they seem so real. Can you assure me, one who goes before, that the way is certain and will lead to only good things for those who love the Most High?"

John laughed. It wasn't just a chuckle but a real guffaw. His eyes also bespoke some sort of merriment that neither I nor Jesus could fathom. "Are you ready to mock me now, Cousin?" Jesus asked with some anger.

"Mock? No, not at all," John said as he sat down beside Jesus on a boulder big enough for two. "Your father says you have had no signs. What do you think those nightmares were? And, sadly, your father is wrong; those visions of the future come not from the devil but from heaven itself."

"And that seems funny to you?" I asked. "Are you truly mad?"

"No, I didn't laugh at the suffering, only that the son of the Most High is seeking angels when he should have understood by now that it is only our suffering and death, mine as surely as his own, that we can expect in this life. And it is a sad truth that for all the generations to come, until the second coming itself, many men and women will do evil things, In Jesus's name, or in the name of many false gods, or some in nobody's name at all, except greed and prejudice and evil themselves. Men will ever find an excuse for their turning away from God, the God who has given them the free will to be so much more than puppets. But God so loves us that he is willing to offer himself up as a sacrifice, offer us up as a sacrifice, in his name. Behold then, cousin Joseph, this man, Jesus of Nazareth, the lamb of God, he who has come to redeem the world."

"The world, all the world?" I questioned. "Aren't we Jews God's chosen people?"

"The Most High chose our people to receive the two great commandments: to love the one true God with one's whole heart and soul and to love one's neighbor as oneself. But these simple commands are too beautiful to be kept to one people. Everyone must have the opportunity to know the one true God and his love. But why am I telling you two all this? Don't you already know?" John asked, switching to a bewildered look more quickly than seemed possible as he stood up. "Can it be possible that you don't both already know?"

"How can I bear all the suffering and hate and lies to be offered in my name?" Jesus asked his cousin. "I'm ready to preach love, to stand up for the poor, to chastise the greedy and the hypocrite, to exalt the lowly and downtrodden, but why do any of it if so many can misunderstand and misuse my message?"

John seemed almost too exasperated to speak further. But I felt something and I took the spot John had abandoned next to Jesus, put my arm around his shoulder and said.

"To justify your parents' lives, that's why, my son. And to justify the lives of all the people, now and forever, who try to do what is pleasing to God. Certainly much good too will come from your message, your example, your love. Isn't that right, John?"

"There is no greater message to be given to man," he answered. "Of course, in your hearts, you must already know this too. But we have to be prepared for great suffering first. And because the nature of this life is to suffer and then to die, Jesus, to be the perfect example for all, must also suffer and die. He has come to the world to deliver us from sin. Are you ready, my cousin, to do what you have been ordained to do?"

"What does it matter whether I'm ready or not?" Jesus said, shaking his head, "if it is ordained, how can I escape?"

"The readiness is everything," John responded. "You must be willing, even as your earthly father was willing to believe in all the things the Most High asked him to believe and suffer. The readiness is all and the reward is great and eternal, remember that."

Jesus rose up with my arm still around him. He gave me an embrace almost as strong as the one John had delivered a few hours before. "Soon I will embrace you father in a departing embrace. You must stay strong to help mother, for she too will suffer greatly. I have to begin the work I was made for, no matter where it leads us on earth, our triumph will be everlasting, even as this prophet proclaims."

John embraced Jesus. Tears lit up his dark eyes and made them seem beatific rather than scary or unbalanced. It was now Jesus's turn to laugh.

"I don't think the Messiah will be able to come as quickly if you break all his bones. Release me, cousin so I can breathe."

We walked back to the home of Elizabeth, where two holy, wonderful women awaited the word that would no longer be held from them or from anyone with the disposition to accept it.

Chapter Twenty-Seven

Jesus stayed in Ain Karin after Passover, stayed with John and Elizabeth so that he and his cousin could talk over what approach Jesus should take in spreading his gospel to the people of Israel. He promised he would visit with us again before heading out. John told him he needed focus and with focus and full conviction would come great power, power he could use to bring his message to all. And so Mary and I returned to Nazareth alone. I explained much of what had transpired when John and I had found Jesus that early evening, but I did not stress the truth of all the suffering ahead. I didn't want to worry Mary more than she was already worried. But Mary was ever wiser than I. She somehow already understood that we had misjudged, like everyone else, what it would mean for the promised Messiah to come. Our son was not destined to overthrow the Roman oppressors or bring the Jewish nation to world prominence, but rather he had come to upset our world even more by insisting on an almost impossible task, that we really love one another as we loved ourselves and that, no matter what happened to us, we would love the Lord with our entire beings, without question. I well understood why Jesus would need to prepare himself with his cousin's aid and support, before heading out on that suicide mission.

Knowing now that Jesus was about to embark on his destined journey and that we had somehow not lived our lives in vain made both Mary and me more hopeful and more at peace. We spent a few months of relative calm and happiness and our affection for each other we expressed in the most subtle but satisfying of ways. Mary visited my shop more often, bringing me a drink or just staying to talk. I found myself more often taking breaks from my work to see what she was up to. When it was time to continue Jesus's ministry to the children and to the poor and infirm, we went together and we distributed more than ever in food, clothing and the toys I tried to construct from what I had seen Jesus create. The more we gave the better we felt; our own material needs lessened as we felt more fulfilled in each other's company. We seemed to want to be together more hours in each day than had ever seemed necessary before. And this woman, this ever virgin, who had so often driven me crazy by her never to be accessed physical beauty, now comforted me with her grace and concern. In some ways, this happy time together seemed like something the Lord owed us, for all he had asked of us for so many years before. If I believed in jinxes, I would probably say that thinking like that is what caused our happy respite to end, when my health suddenly began to decline.

The first thing I noticed was a sore throat. I'd always been someone who avoided frequent colds and eating a simple healthy diet with much exercise had always kept me pretty fit. Still, having a sore throat wasn't new to me, so I wasn't concerned at all until after ten days instead of the soreness going away it got a little worse. Over the following weeks it got worse still and it even began to feel like there was something growing down in my throat, and I started to have trouble with a near constant cough and even some trouble with breathing, especially at night. I still was hoping for the best and praying for some heavenly aid or intercession, but when I got still a little worse Mary insisted that I go see a physician. I didn't have a lot of confidence in their abilities, maybe because I had never before gone to one in my life, but this fellow had been kind and patient with Joachim during his last days, so I trusted him enough to make a visit.

The man, whose name was David, was not much older than Jesus, but he had a way about him that made you feel he was much older. He took as good a look down my throat as he could manage and I could tell right away that he did not like what he was seeing, though he tried to shield me from his concern at first. I didn't see any use in that:

"Is it something bad, doctor? Something serious? I need to know."

Young David looked at me with a real look of compassion. That look, though I appreciated its kindness, told me all I really needed to know. Still, I listened.

"You have what the first great physician, the Greek Hippocrates, calls a cancer, which is the Greek word for a crab. It's like a living thing, pinching you and growing larger by the day. There's nothing we can do to diminish it. If it continues to grow, I'm afraid you won't survive it. Of course, whatever the Lord decrees will happen; one should never entirely lose hope."

"So that's why a crab isn't kosher, eh doctor?" I tried to joke.

"That's right," he nodded. "Our forefathers knew what to forbid. I wish I had the power so easily to forbid this one that has found a home where we can't get it to go away. I'm sorry to bring you such bad news."

"You are just the messenger; the bad news had already arrived." I said as I patted him on the shoulder. "It's always better to know."

The pain was one thing. Each day it got more difficult to swallow and even to talk, and my voice, which had always been a point of pride for its resonance and deep tones, became scratchy and halting. More importantly, I was in a panic over leaving Mary alone. Jesus was bound for much travel and a sad end; what would Mary do for survival if I died and how could she deal with what would happen to Jesus without me to help her? Such an innocent, loving and faithful woman should not have to spend her last days as a widow whose child was going to die some horrible death. I prayed and prayed for the miracle the doctor suggested as my only chance. Mary prayed too and tried to keep a happy countenance in front of me, though I heard her more than once weeping, alone in our bedroom, when she didn't know I had come back into the house and could hear her. I thought to try to console her, but I didn't want her to know I knew she was not holding up as well as she pretended to.

In the midst of this trouble Jesus returned. He was practically glowing with a new found confidence and conviction, but that turned to concern when he heard of my misfortune. My voice was much altered by now and I'd lost some weight, so there was no sense in trying to pretend I was fine. We prayed together and certainly those prayers and just having him back home did make me feel a little better. It was getting more difficult to eat, though, and so Mary tried her best to make soups and give me soft foods I could still swallow. Jesus had planned only to stay a few days before heading for Capernaum, where he had already begun to do some preaching during his fishing days and where he had made many friends; this seemed to him like an apt place to begin his ministry, but his concern for me and for his mother, kept him by our side for weeks.

There was a wedding feast planned at nearby Cana, where one of Mary's cousins was to be wed. Mary liked this cousin well but they were not particularly close and so she just thought she would skip the feast and stay home with me. I encouraged her instead to at least attend a part of it and to take Jesus with her; I told them I'd be fine by myself for a few days.

"Don't be crazy, Joseph," my wife admonished me. "How could I enjoy a wedding feast knowing how you would be suffering here?"

"It's not like I'm a cripple or don't know how to heat up soup," I responded. "The pain won't be greater or smaller depending on your presence or absence. I would feel better knowing you are at a celebration, spending time with your only son. I promise I'll be here waiting to hear all about it when you both return."

And so they went, once they understood I really wanted them to go. For some reason I really wanted this time alone, to try to figure out how I could help Mary get through life without me and to try to help Jesus not feel guilty in leaving his mother behind. I prayed and I thought and I prayed some more, but instead of relief or a solution I only got worse pain, pain now extending to other parts of the body besides the throat, trouble with my urination, pains in my head and hands, pain that made me doubt again that there could be a loving God. But I offered up all my suffering to that very God, if only he would protect my wife and son from despair and want and failure. And still I received no answer, just more pain.

That night I put out my lantern, I know I did, before trying to sleep, but when I awoke, in the dead of night, the lantern was shining, almost directly in my face. Soon I understood why; it was the Angel Solomon, whose friends called him Shlomo, who had returned, though at first I didn't recognize him, since he was no longer disheveled and looked, dared I to think so, almost radiant? As always, he knew my thoughts.

"Still no wings though, my old friend; I had to draw the line somewhere. But my radiance reflects your own, and how you have grown in faith and obedience to the will of the Most High."

"Have I really been pleasing to our Lord of hosts?" I asked.

"Joseph the Craftsman, you've been praying up such a storm, as you suffer great pain, but all for the sake of others not for yourself at all. The Lord is impressed. So impressed he has given me permission to relieve you of much of your suffering."

"Much but not all?" I almost chuckled, figuring I was just in another dream anyway. "I guess I'll have to take what I can get."

"And still a sense of humor, too? You've grown much since last we met, Joseph. But this is no dream, and what I have to tell you, must remain between us until you reach your final reward."

I sat up in bed, the pain had not diminished even a little, but I nodded to let my angel friend know I was listening.

"First, I have to tell you, there's no cure for your physical pain I can give you. It's been ordained that you should leave this earth soon, and no mortal man can stop living without a good reason. You now have yours."

"Yes, I've often heard there's no good way to die. This one seems particularly bad, but what do I know, I've never died before. Still, it's not my death that worries me, Mr. Angel, but rather what will happen to Mary. Why can't I be here to protect her from all the suffering ahead or at least suffer it with her? Why can't I be here to help Jesus should he need me in his moments of crisis? It doesn't seem fair after all I've done, to take me from my post now."

"Joseph, you know about the suffering to come. So it has been ordained. But Jesus will not suffer just for the sake of suffering and surely not in vain. Jesus's death, though as painful as any mortal man must suffer, will be a triumph, for I am here to tell you, he will rise again."

"Yes, he'll rise to paradise, I know, but,…"

"No, my craftsman friend, he will rise, on the third day, in fulfillment of the scriptures. He will take from death all its power; he will return to comfort his mother's tears and to buoy his disciples with renewed purpose. All this I tell you, Joseph as a special gift, one you have well-earned because you have pleased God well and he wants your death too to be in peace and glory, knowing what is to come."

Shlomo told me these truths not in his usual smug or sarcastic or slightly condescending tone, but with real compassion and concern for me, reminding me of the doctor's appointment of a few weeks before. "Could an angel have compassion, shed tears even for a mere sinner like me?"

"Yes, of course, my friend," the angel answered my thoughts, "since you have suffered much, been asked to believe what no man before you has been asked to believe, of course I can feel for you. And though you had your many moments of sin and doubt, you have made us all proud. And so I'm privileged to share with you what few men are ever given to know, the future."

"And this future will be glorious for Jesus?"

"Yes, certainly, but also for you. You, Joseph the craftsman will be remembered, by millions and millions of good men and women forever."

"I? I will be remembered?" I asked, my voice scratchy but now tinged with surprise and wonder. "Who will possibly remember me?"

"Who won't?" he asked with a tone more like his usual self. "In the years to come the men and women who have lived lives most pleasing to God will be called saints. And you will be always remembered as one of the most important, the patron of not only fathers, but even of expectant mothers. Of travelers, immigrants, people who buy and sell houses, not only of craftsmen but of all workers. Many

centuries from now, the church founded in Jesus's name will declare you the patron of that church itself. Not only that, but entire countries, countries that don't
even exist yet, you will also be their patron."

"How can this be?" I asked astonished. "Surely this must be a dream."

"Is the pain you feel a dream? It feels real enough, doesn't it? Dream or no,
every word I am telling you is true. And why not? You have been an ideal father,
loving your son even when you knew he wasn't your own, loving him even as you
doubted everything else around you, even as you had to travel to a foreign land
and then return when the Lord demanded it. And you became, finally, an ideal
husband, overcoming your own sinful nature to be dedicated to the ways of the
Lord and of the Holy Spirit. And you have been an excellent, honest and skilled
worker, making your very work an example to your son and to your community.
And now you sit here, full of pain I can only imagine, caring nothing for yourself
and only for your wife and child. Of course you will be remembered and reverenced forever; with your wife and child forever revered as 'The Holy Family.'"

"Thank you, thank you, for these gifts. If even only a bit of this would come
true, I would be honored beyond all unworthiness. But, still, I ask for your patience. How will Mary fare without me?"

"Soon Jesus will become a phenomenon, the greatest speaker of wisdom and
truth the world will ever come to know. And he will attract many disciples. Some
one or more of them will ever be able to make sure his mother has enough to
survive, and Jesus will remain in touch with her as a loving son should. His death
will pierce her like a sword, even as the old man predicted at the child's presentation, but her faith will be unwavering and her ultimate joy and triumph just a
matter of hours away from that agony. And Mary herself even as she was born
without sin, will not suffer the corruption of the body but will be assumed into
Paradise, as another special sign of her worthiness to be the mother of God. She
will be reverenced forever after too, as befitting of her status as the holy, loving
mother of Jesus and the only woman born without sin. Don't worry about your
family, Joseph. They will suffer much, as all on earth must suffer, but their glory
and triumph will be eternal, even as your own shall be."

"This is all so incredible," I rasped, overcome both with pain and amazement.
"How can all this happen to me?" I asked, though I could feel in my surging happiness that it was all true knowing as I did that angels could not lie.

"There's even more," Shlomo laughed. "You know the Romans, who are so haughty and high-handed now. It won't be long before practically everyone in Rome has become a Jesus follower, a lot of them not as devoted as they should be, but still. And all through the region once ruled by Rome, the place they will call Italy, you'll be honored and remembered. In fact, they're going to make a special confection, better even than Elizabeth's honey cakes, for the day each year that they assign to honor you; there are going to be festivals and parades, not just in Italy but all over. And they'll be so many cities and towns and rivers and children named after you it will make your head spin. If you weren't destined to be a saint it might make you pretty full of yourself, craftsman. Remember to stay humble, okay?"

"Yes, I will," I said, as it seemed he was preparing to leave. I added quickly, "But why have you waited so long to tell me all this? Why all these years between visits? Why didn't Jesus himself ever get a nod from above to let him know his path sooner? Why…"

"I can't tell you why, exactly, I'm not God, after all, right? I can tell you this, though. Jesus will perform many signs, miraculous cures and other things that will make his fish finding seem like nothing. But these hard-hearted people, with all these signs, will still betray him in the end. And so I think the Lord knows that those who will follow must follow without signs. For who would not be thankful to a God who cured their cancer, who brought their child back from death, who undid their leprosy? But God needs us to trust and love even when the child dies or the cancer kills. This gift I give to you no one else can have and you are only receiving it as you leave this veil of tears. But you also are destined to be the patron of a 'happy death,' and so your gift I have brought you is to know while you still breathe, the great things that are to come. And this is a gift that God will withhold from all others, who will have to count on their faith alone to know."

With that the Angel Shlomo gave me a bit of a smile and then departed, in his favorite purple smoke mode. I found that I was wholly awake; there was no dream to return from. And I found my pain just as forceful as ever, though now it was precious to me, exquisite even, as it was my path to all the joy awaiting me.

Chapter Twenty-Eight

Mary returned from Cana with an amazing story to tell.

"Jesus turned water into wine," Mary reported to me as I lay in my bed, too weak now even to get up to greet my family.

I nodded and smiled and asked in an ever more raspy voice: "Why did he do that?"

"Well," Mary continued, "It seems my cousin didn't plan for how thirsty all his guests would be; he thought he had secured enough wine for a small army, but the celebration lasted longer than he figured and while most of the guests still remained he realized he was out of wine. I felt so badly for him; I didn't want him to be disgraced in front of his bride and her family, so I turned to Jesus and told him he had to help them."

"And what did he say?" I asked.

"At first he said it wasn't his time yet, but I knew that he could not go on saying such things forever, so I just told them to do whatever he asked them to do and he gave me a bit of a look, not a roll of the eyes exactly, but still to let me know this was not what he needed just yet, but, like the good son he's always been, he did what I asked and before I knew it, there was plenty of wine for everyone again and I overheard the head steward tell my cousin, 'Why in the world did you keep back the best wine till now? Most of these people are too into their cups to appreciate the difference.'"

"I suppose this amazed everyone present."

"No one was the wiser except my cousin and the few people who carted the water turned into wine over to where the party was. And Jesus didn't want anyone else to know."

"What an odd first sign," I said, with a shake of my head.

"There's nothing odd in our son listening to his mother and having compassion for his cousin. They are both good boys."

"They are both men," I corrected.

"Boys to their mothers always, and good ones," Mary smiled. "But, Joseph, have you been all right? You seem, I'm sad to say, still a little weaker. But really, the reason I rushed in to tell you about the wine, well, I was thinking, if Jesus has come into his powers, is ready to give signs of his glory, what better sign than to restore the health of his own earthly father?"

I could see how optimistic this idea had made Mary. And I felt blessed to know her love was still so directed towards me, who had so often failed her. I didn't respond directly to her suggestion but merely asked, "And where is Jesus now? Didn't he escort you back here to Nazareth?"

"Oh, yes, he's here. Do you want me to call him in?"

"Yes, would you?"

"Of course," Mary said and before she left to get our son she kissed my forehead and smiled, confident that I would soon be well.

Jesus entered our bedroom and greeted me with real concern, concern that heightened once he had a closer look at how I had gone further towards death even in the few days they had been absent from home.

"Father, do you need anything? Perhaps it was wrong of us to leave you here. Should I send for the physician?"

"No earthly doctor can help me now, my son. What most I need is to see you both at my side one last time."

"One last time?" Mary repeated with alarm. "Don't be crazy, Joseph. Let us tell Jesus what we were thinking. Surely, it is right to ask and surely all things are possible with God."

My voice seemed to be fading even as I spoke and speaking itself was now causing me some pain, but I tried to articulate my words as clearly as possible: "Your mother has a notion that you could cure me now, my son, since you've discovered this ability to transform water into wine, why not the sick back to wellness? I have no doubt but that you could do so, but it is best you save your miracles for those who need them; my faith is already secure and I know what must be must be."

"Your eyes, father, are weighted with wisdom, even more so now than in all the years you have helped to guide my path. If this is farewell it is not goodbye. And I promise you I will see to all the needs of my mother, even if I cannot always or even often be with her in person."

"Must I bear this too then? Losing first my father and now the only two other men in my life who I have known well enough fully to love completely? Can a loving God ask so much of his handmaiden?" Mary asked.

I wanted to tell Mary all that the angel had shared with me. I wanted to tell her of how I, unworthy as I have always been, was not only headed for an eternal reward in the next life, but was also going to be honored and loved for countless generations in the world I was departing. I wanted to tell her too that she would be even more venerated and loved by those generations. I knew two things, though: one, that Mary would not care about any veneration she was set to receive and two, that I could not share the secrets the angel had bestowed on me precisely because of my weakness; Mary would bear her suffering ahead with faith and dignity and would never waver. Her only concern was for others and she would live to see Jesus resurrected and justified and, knowing that, I had compassion for her but no ultimate worry. Angels could not lie nor could the faith and happiness that was surging within me, almost enough to convince me for a moment that I was again fully well.

"Forgive me, both of you, for not always being the best husband or father. Know that my love was always greater than my ability to express it or to act as a better man might have."

"You were chosen by God himself to be my spouse; I knew who you were the first moment I saw you and I have only thankfulness for the strength and love you have given to us both all these years. No one can be perfect, but you, Joseph, have always been pure of heart."

"And blessed are the pure in heart," Jesus added, "for they will see God."

"Yes, and soon," I said, with the best smile I could manage.

Mary began to weep; Jesus put his arm around her shoulder and tried to comfort her. Mary was wrong, of course. Though most everyone who has ever walked the earth has found it impossible to be perfect, I had spent the last thirty years or so with the only two people who were. Both of them were born without sin; both of them had kept themselves truly "pure of heart" for all of their lives. They were God's representatives on earth; they were the proof that the Lord loved his people and was willing even to let his only son suffer as all mortals must suffer, for the sake of our redemption. I had been asked to be a kind of odd reminder to them that no one else was like them, that men were inclined to sin, as part of their free will, and only with doubt and at times even despair could they be truly challenged in their goodness. I understood now, as completely as an imperfect man could, that even as Mary had modeled Jesus's heavenly nature to him, it had been my role to model what it meant to be a normal human being and much of what was good and understanding and sympathetic about Jesus had been helped along by my imperfect example. The Most High truly worked enshrouded in mystery, but I now knew it had all been necessary and it had all been worth it. Though sad to leave Mary behind for a time and sadder still to know the suffering that lay ahead for my family, knowing what was to come would enable me to have that "happy death."

"I know you'll remember your promise to care for your mother," I said to Jesus as I reached for his hand. "And, Mary, never doubt but that my love for you exceeded my ability to express it, but I know now the greatest gift that the Lord could have given me was to spend these years with you."

I reached with my other hand for Mary and she took my hand and kissed it, her tears touching my skin as she did so. With one hand holding the hand of the most blessed of mothers and the other holding the hand of the very Son of God, I felt myself the luckiest man who had ever tried to prepare himself for his final moments. I felt blessed. I felt perfectly blessed.

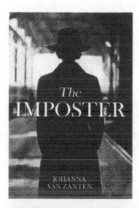

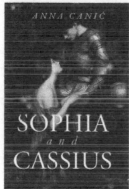